BULLARD'S BEAUTY

Bullard's Battle
Book #8

Dale Mayer

Books in This Series:

BULLARD'S BEAUTY (BULLARD'S BATTLE, BOOK 8)
Dale Mayer
Valley Publishing

ISBN-13: 978-1-773363-40-0
Print Edition

Books in This Series:

About This Book

Welcome to a new stand-alone but interconnected series from Dale Mayer. This is Bullard's story—and that of his team's. All raw, rough, incredibly capable men who have one goal: to find out who was behind the attack on their leader, before the attacker, or attackers, return to finish the job.

Stay tuned for more nonstop action as the men narrow down their suspects ... and find a way to let love back into their own empty lives.

Bullard's barely aware of his surroundings, as he slowly emerges from a coma and months of slow healing. He recognizes the general area but not the facilities or the woman attending him. Neither does he remember exactly what happened.

Leia, a gifted surgeon in her own right, hadn't expected this giant of a man to wash up in the shallows by her beach, nor to call on every trick she's ever learned to keep him alive. Her instincts tell her to take a leave, to keep him hidden, even as she struggles to answer his questions. The longer he's with her, the more she realizes how hard it could be to let him go. But he has turned the corner and is healing quickly.

Only the real world intrudes faster than expected, as one of Bullard's team shows up on her beach, bringing others, who'd been watching and waiting for the team to find Bullard for them—and now swoop in for the kill ...

Sign up to be notified of all Dale's releases here!

https://smarturl.it/DaleNews

CHAPTER 1

B ULLARD OPENED HIS eyes to stare up at the mosquito netting all around him. He could almost be at one of his African compounds with that netting, but what he saw out the long curtains that acted as doors was a white beach and a blue ocean. He wasn't in Africa; he was in the South Pacific.

But he didn't know a whole lot else. His brain was a jumble of fragmented images and voices. His nightmares were so ugly that he shuddered as he relived them. Some he could place; some he couldn't. He knew some were experiences he'd had in the US Navy. Others were missions from his own company.

He knew he had his own company but couldn't access the details of who worked for him. It was a sad state of affairs, but the good part was the certainty that this Swiss cheese brain of his was filling in, slowly but surely. He didn't even know how long he'd been here. Weeks perhaps, even months. The days had rolled into this incessant darkness, with intermittent moments of light. Every time he woke up, the same woman was here.

Her name was Leia, and he had no reason to disbelieve her. She also hadn't offered a last name. However she had been constantly at his side. When he was sick, when he couldn't do more than roll over and upchuck, she held a bowl to his chin. She held food and drink to his lips, encouraging him to swallow. She'd been here constantly, a guiding light in the darkness of his world. He didn't know a thing about her beyond the little bit she'd given him. But he couldn't tell her anything about himself in return.

Whenever he asked for information about her, she smiled and told him that, as soon as he gave her some information, she would give him some. He'd racked his brains for days to come up with something, and eventually one little piece came up. As soon as he told her, she'd given him another piece of her life. He knew what she was doing and why, but it was still frustrating. Yet it was no more frustrating than everything else in his world. Not knowing what had happened was difficult. He had an idea that he'd been piecing together, but he had no details.

He was desperate to have those details.

She didn't seem to know very much, only telling him that, as far as she knew, he'd been in a bad accident. That fact was evident, so he didn't need her confirmation on that. What he didn't know was if it was truly an accident or something targeted. The fact that he could even think about a targeted attack—plus the random words that floated through his head all the time—meant that he had something to do with security and probably a whole lot more, if his memories were anything to go by. It was a scary world out there, and apparently he'd lived in it.

Thrived in it.

He could only hope he was on the good side. It didn't feel right to be on the wrong side, but he also knew that severe injuries like this could result in incredible traumatic physical damage and sometimes even personality changes. He didn't know what kind of an asshole he was before this, but he sure as hell hoped he was a better one afterward.

Another woman kept drifting in and out of his head too.

Somebody tall and blonde, with a Viking warrior look. But he had no name to go with her, just a softness in his heart when he thought of her. And that was of no help because he didn't know if she was his wife, an ex-wife, or even somebody he'd cared about who had passed on. A sense of cotton batting hung around her, as if he needed to protect the memory.

He didn't understand that either. Nothing made sense, and the more he struggled, the more frustrated he got, prompting Leia to tell him to calm down and to just let things happen naturally. But then her memories hadn't been sacrificed. Her body wasn't lying here broken, barely able to do anything, even though he had made great improvements. She told him one time that it wasn't his body that was broken as much as what had happened to his brain and that he would heal, but it would take time.

And she'd given him that mysterious look, like she knew something he didn't, and she wouldn't share. And again that drove him crazy, but he didn't think she was out to be mean. He thought it was more that she didn't think he was ready to hear the truth. He also knew that he'd had surgery, likely more than one because he had stitches, but he didn't know what corrective steps had been taken.

And she wasn't talking. When he'd asked, she'd said that some measures had been needed to keep him alive. He could understand that, and, at the time, he'd had enough sense to keep quiet about it. He was alive; that was the main thing. And, once he was stable, many other things could be fixed eventually. He just needed time in order to get things cleared up.

None of it made a whole lot of sense, but, as he woke that next morning, he found more clarity in his heart; his brain was less fuzzy, his thoughts clearer. As Leia walked in to check on him, he smiled. "This is getting to be a habit," he said.

"It's been a habit for quite a while now." Her peaceful countenance was something he found soothing and refreshing. "Are you hungry?

"Actually I am," he whispered. "I'm not sure why though."

"It's a good sign," she said, her gaze ever watchful.

"I'm fine, you know?" he said, when she finally raised her gaze to study his features.

"I can see that," she said, her eyes crinkling up. He could never say a harsh word to her, as it would be like pulling wings off a butterfly. But as gentle and as fragile as she seemed, he knew she had a steel core because he hadn't been easy to look after in the initial days, and yet she'd hung in there. She hadn't given an inch, and she hadn't let him have his way over anything. So he had to conclude that she was ruling with a velvet glove, and, for whatever reason, he was letting her. Mostly because he was currently a prisoner, ... imprisoned by a broken body and a broken mind that needed yet more time.

"Anything else from your medicine woman?"

"So today you call her a *medicine woman* instead of a *witch doctor*?" she asked, clearly teasing. Her voice was like a cool breeze on a hot day. Refreshing and so soothing that it made his heart ache for something so different. He said softly, "I'll call her whatever I need to in order to get the answers I need."

"So driven," she murmured.

4

"You know it," he said, nodding.

"I can see it," she said. "Every day you've been driving yourself hard, pushing to get back to full strength."

"I'd be happy to get back to having a full set of brains," he said. "I feel like somebody took mine and shook them, until they looked like spaghetti, and now I'm left trying to hook them back up into a normal brain pattern."

She chuckled softly. "That's not a bad description," she said. "But that doesn't mean you're necessarily ready for more though. The brain protects itself, and, when it can handle more, it will give you more."

"Then my brain needs to get a better understanding of who I am," he snapped, "because I want it now."

With the softest of smiles, she headed out of the room.

He groaned. "Sorry. I don't mean to take it out on you."

"I know," she said in that same gentle voice.

He just sighed. Anytime he raised his voice or talked to her in anything other than his gentlest voice, she would quietly withdraw her presence. He knew it was likely the result of some kind of training, but he didn't understand. It was almost like he'd ended up in some monastery, and she had these rules about how she was willing to be treated.

The thing is, her tactics worked, and he always felt like a heel whenever he raised his voice. It didn't matter how frustrated he was, just something was seriously special about her. And, even though he'd apologized, it would still take a while before she returned. He could try to convince her to come back, but it never worked, or at least it hadn't so far.

When she returned this time, he frowned as he stared out of the window. "Any chance of going down to the beach?"

She spoke quietly. "Maybe this afternoon."

5

"Good," he said, with a note of satisfaction. "It looks awesome out there."

"It is," she said. "It's beautiful."

"How long have you been here?" he asked.

"How long have you been here?" she replied, with her usual parry back.

He glared at her. "At least eight weeks," he said.

"You're right," she said. "I've been here at least five years."

"But only five years, so you weren't born here, huh?"

"Where were you born?" she immediately responded.

He groaned. "In Germany, I think," he said, looking pensive as he stared outside. "But I don't think I was there very long."

"Any idea why?"

"My parents," he said. "Something happened to my mother."

"And that caused your father to do something different?" she murmured.

"It did," he said quietly. "Hard to get all the details though."

"Maybe, but you're doing so much better," she said, always with that soft smile of hers.

He smiled back at her. "You are such a cheerleader."

"I call it as I see it," she said, with that same gentleness. When she walked out the next time, he hoped it was to get him food. He was never one to sit and to be waited on, but, in his current condition, he didn't have much choice. He thought that he was somebody who liked to cook, but he didn't have any proof of that, just that his mind dredged up really good meals that he'd had. He wasn't sure if he had done the cooking, but he had the feeling that he was a capable hand at a lot of things.

Now if only he knew where that training had come from or just what those skills actually were. Just then, the same blond woman drifted through his mind again. He shook his head. "I'm not sure who you are," he said, "but we're close. Are you upset at me being missing, or were you already gone first?" Of course nobody could answer his questions as he lay here, but he thought about the old seer woman on the island that he called the witch doctor.

She'd come in a couple times, and clearly she didn't like him much, although she had been open about his future, which hadn't looked positive. She said that he was being hunted, that people were looking for him. Something sounded really familiar about that, and, while he could accept her analysis, he didn't understand any of the details. He didn't think she would provide him with any of them either. She wasn't even sure what she was doing here. But she kept coming back, sometimes with weird comments.

Like this Terkel character. Bullard wasn't sure if anyone named Terkel was after him or what the reason was or even if it were true. What had Bullard done to warrant being hunted? Funny how Leia had used that *hunted* word as well. It was almost like these two women had some kind of inner communication system or a line to the outside world that they weren't sharing with him. That would piss him off if he found out they had access to a comm that they hadn't told him about.

Apparently they had no phones of any kind, and Leia hadn't been to the mainland in a long time. He wondered at a woman so obviously content to be where she was.

Not much was here. At least nothing he saw, but again he didn't know if she was keeping anything from him. It wouldn't surprise him in a way, but he hoped not. A part of him didn't want her to be keeping things from him; yet that was also selfish on his part because he was keeping a lot from her, just not by choice. He called out to her. "Leia?"

"I'm coming with food in a few minutes," she said.

"Thank you."

And he shifted again. One of the things he really wanted to do was get back on his feet, so he didn't have to ask for assistance to the bathroom. A big man like him shouldn't be brought down by something so simple as bodily functions, but, at the moment, there was really no other way. Or was there? He slowly pushed himself to a sitting position on the edge of the bed, wincing at the newly healed shoulder joints that had taken such a bashing. He had a broken leg, which was splinted and had a rough cast. It was doing much better. Leia had said she'd look at it a little bit later to see if the cast could come off, so they could start working to get that leg more flexible.

And also something was happening with his ribs and his spine, which he sure-as-hell felt. Everything seemed to poke and to prod and to push at him, as if he had a live wire inside. He wasn't even sure what else was going on, except for his head injury. He reached up and felt the full line of stitches across his skull. The actual stitches were gone by now of course. Just puckered skin remained, which said a lot about how long he'd been here. He wondered if everybody in his life had given up on him. That would be hard too.

He sighed as he sat here for a long moment, then decided he would try to get up again. He noted a pair of crutches leaning against the end of the bad. He frowned at that, wondering how Leia had known.

Sometimes he swore to God that Leia was a witch herself. Grabbing the crutches and moving very slowly, he pushed himself to his feet and hobbled to the simple makeshift outhouse. As soon as he was done, he stood, shaky and weaving ever-so-slightly. As he tried to remain upright, he studied what looked to him like a Pacific island. Completely uninhabited, he saw no sign of anyone, except for the little hut he was in. A little farther back was another hut, a cabinet-looking thing, and he wondered if that was Leia's.

LEIA STEPPED OUT on her deck, as she studied her patient standing outside the small outhouse. He looked weak but actually quite improved over how she'd seen him for the last few weeks. The fact that he had made it to the facilities on his own was huge. She had plumbing up here, but it was still very primitive. She lived on an island completely away from the rest of the world, and that was how she liked it.

When she had finally managed to drag her sorry butt here, she'd been a broken piece of humanity and had desperately needed the solace that a place like this could bring. When she'd found him in the water, while she was out fishing, she knew exactly what he needed. She was a surgeon and had been a damn good one. Right up until a series of unfortunate events had cost her everything—her job, her self-confidence, and all the people she'd spent so much time trying to help. Now that all seemed like a long time ago. It wasn't so far removed from the present, but still it was a lifetime away.

She wouldn't ever return to that kind of workforce environment again. She'd spent her life helping people, but, when it turned out badly, it seemed like everyone in her world had turned on her. As for her current patient, she didn't know what his story was, but something was there. Something terribly dark. She'd been there beside him through all his nightmares, hearing the fear and the night terrors that ripped through him. She didn't know what had happened in his world, but it was still happening, of that she had no doubt. She'd heard through the grapevine that people were looking for him, but, so far, they hadn't found her patient or Leia.

She kept in touch with the outside world but didn't know who to trust on this. She had no idea who was the right person to inform. She had done as much surgery on him as she could, trying to repair the injuries and to keep his body as functional as possible. Considering her island ER setup, she had done a hell of a job, if she did say so herself. This Terkel person though, that was a different story entirely. The old medicine woman on the other side of the island said that Terkel kept contacting her with a message to tell her patient that Terkel was looking for him, and now he'd found him. *Bullard.*

She half expected that her idyllic island life would get completely disrupted by the arrival of foreigners in connection with Bullard. What would she do then?

Her heart ached at the thought of him leaving, but of course he would. This wasn't his world or where he'd chosen to spend his life. He'd gotten here by chance. Something had happened that had put him on this pathway, and she'd done her best to rescue him, then to get him healthy and able to go home. He was far from 100 percent, but every day he made visible improvements. As he gradually regained his strength, she had begun to see the powerhouse of the man that he was. And she knew that, as soon as he fully understood what was going on, he would be chomping at the bit to head back to his real life.

She would miss him terribly.

She wasn't sure who this Ice person was or several other people Bullard kept calling out for. The names didn't mean anything to her, and Leia had no way of knowing whether they did to him or not. She'd written them down but was still uncertain at what point in time she should ask him about it. She didn't want to set him back any further. And he had already proven to be wily and difficult to handle when he had his mind set on a particular course. She figured that, once he approached anything near his full strength, he would be almost impossible to keep down.

At that point she would have lost control over his care. She knew that time was coming, but it would still be hard to let go. She didn't want to admit it, but she had become more than attached. He was a special patient, perhaps because he was the first one she'd looked after in all these years, but he'd also been so broken and so desperately in need that it was a true challenge for her talents. For the longest time she'd had nobody for that part of her psyche to deal with, then suddenly ended up with somebody who needed her desperately, and she'd given him her all. Was it enough? She didn't know, especially considering she had no idea what was going on in his world, including how he had ended up in the ocean and so terribly injured.

Was he in danger? She suspected as much, since the medicine woman had warned Leia that Bullard had bad enemies and needed help. Well, the help part she understood; it was just a matter of what she was supposed to do at this point, recognizing her options were limited. He was a good man, at least what she had seen of him. Her heart told her that he was a very strong and a very tough man, but he was also a man of honor.

Maybe that was just wishful thinking because she needed something to believe in, and he was it. She nodded, as she stepped back inside her cabin, knowing that he'd seen the movement. He'd been completely cooped up in that small space down there for too long. It started out as basically her writing space, a little gazebo without walls that she had erected for her own purpose. A place slightly separate from her home that she needed for working out, writing, and yoga, just to release the strain and the stress inside her own system. As soon as the food was ready, she loaded up his and her platters, then carried them carefully to where he rested on the bed once again.

"You have your own space," he growled.

She nodded. "Of course."

"There's no *of course* about it," he said.

He sounded aggrieved, as if she'd kept something important from him. She just smiled. "You're being foolish," she said. "My life has been here for a long time, so obviously this little hut isn't where I made my home."

"I know," he said, suddenly sounding bashful.

She chuckled. "You can't seem to decide whether you'll behave as a little boy or as a man."

"Because, for the first time, it feels like the little boy in me is being allowed to come out," he confessed.

CHAPTER 2

L EIA LOOKED AT him, then chuckled. "Nothing wrong with that," she murmured. "We all need moments of peace and quiet to let out our inner child."

"If you say so." He looked at the food and grinned. "Did you catch the fish today?"

"Not today," she said easily. "I'm still not the fisherman others on the island are."

"I imagine it's a lifestyle for them," he said.

"I guess so," she said. "Still I get a little bit every time I go out. It's just not quite enough."

"Looks like you get everything you need here though."

"To a certain extent I do. Yes."

"And do you want to stay here?"

The question threw her. She lifted her dark gaze to his and studied him, wondering what was behind the question. "I don't know," she said. "I haven't been here all my life, so I do know what the rest of the world looks like. I can't say that I'm in great favor of what the world has to offer sometimes."

He nodded in understanding. "You've seen some of the worst of it, haven't you?"

"I don't know that I would say that," she said gently. "I think a lot of the worst of it out there is the people them-selves."

"Always is," he said.

She gave him his plate, a towel for his fingers, and a fork. He dove in with an appetite that surprised her. "You really are feeling better, aren't you?" she said, with a pleased grin.

"I am. It's just this damn brain."

"That damn brain has held you in good stead. Cut it some slack." He gave her a one-arm shrug. She looked at him and asked, "Anything coming back?"

"Not that I can make sense of." He shook his head. "Just lots of memories that aren't very pleasant."

"Of course." She nodded.

"No 'of course' about it," he said. "It would be nice if I had some meaning to it all."

"There is, and there will be." She shrugged. "You just have to give it a chance."

"I know," he said, "but it's frustrating nonetheless."

"Remember. Your brain must heal too."

"I know. I know," he growled, showing his palms. "The trouble is, I can't hurry up the healing process."

"You can practice patience." She tucked into her meal, but her gaze was wary. He was healing faster than she had expected, was gaining strength at a phenomenal rate. Once his brain decided to kick in fully, he would charge forward, hell-bent for leather, regardless of what she had to say.

He moved his injured leg around. "I was happy to see it held my weight."

"You've also lost a lot of weight," she murmured.

"Not because of the food though," he said, with great satisfaction, as he stared down at his plate. "It's very simple, but it tastes good and is very filling."

"It's also good for you. Not all food is the same."

"No, and I like this," he said with a nod.

"Good," she replied, as she reached for his empty plate.

"Would you like some coffee now?"

"Coffee sounds great, but could we go outside?" he asked hopefully.

She knew at this point he could probably get there on his own, but he was looking for her permission. And, with that, she nodded. "We can probably get you to the edge of the beach, if you like."

"I'd like to go in the water and swim, but I know the ocean tides would tire me easily."

"A set of pools are to the side," she said. "If you could get yourself there, you'd probably be okay."

"So we're not going to the beach?"

"The adjacent pools are fresh water that runs into the ocean," she said. "The water would be cooler, but it would be easier for you to get in and out."

He looked at the ocean. "It doesn't look like it would be hard to get in there, but I'm afraid it might be hard to get out."

"You're right," she said. "Sometimes I struggle with it myself. What do you think? Shall we give the pools a try?"

He nodded, then struggled to sit on the side of the bed again. Then, reaching for the crutches, he slowly stood. She gathered the dishes and walked to the big porch deck of the other hut and added the dishes to a bucket of water on the porch. She slept inside under the roof, which covered about three-quarters of the building; the rest opened to the deck area outside. She pointed to the small group of trees about one hundred yards away. "The water comes into a pool there, and I have steps down into it."

"You swim there?"

"I bathe there all the time," she admitted.

He tilted his head. "Good, then show me the way."

As he slowly walked toward the area, she kept a tight eye on his progress. She knew he would assume he could go farther and better than anybody. And, sure enough, it wasn't long before he made it partway, then stopped and looked at her. "You don't have far to go," she said. "Once you're there, you can rest."

"How far?" he asked. "It's looking farther all the time."

"It always does," she said.

He pushed forward, and, when he stopped at the trees, she had really meant it when she said she had a lot of rock ledges going down to the pool. Using the crutches on the dry rocks, he slowly made his way to the water's edge, where she had placed more rocks on the side. He looked at the water, then at her. "Is there any reason not to fall in?"

"Go for it," she said. "It's all safe. But let me take that makeshift cast off first." With that done, he turned, dropped his crutches, and literally fell into the water, causing a great big wave to wash up.

She waited nervously, until he popped to the surface again, but he was obviously half fish because he rolled and twisted as he swam with joy. She laughed at him. "If I'd realized this is what your heart wanted," she said, "I would have gotten you here sooner."

"No, I had to come on my own," he said. "I'm too big for you to manhandle this far, which meant I still had to improve first."

"But look at how well you're doing," she said. "It's amazing how much more range of motion you have with the buoyancy of the water helping out. You're not showing near as much pain as you would if you were trying to twist that way out of the water."

He rolled over on his back, and, with a great big sigh, he

floated. "The current isn't bad either," he marveled.

"No, not here," she said. "It's quite calm." After he was out of the water and stretched out one of the rocks, still wearing only his shorts, she asked, "Are you okay here while I go put on coffee?"

"Are you okay if I just sleep here?"

She laughed, then leaned over, checked his forehead. "I'm fine if you do that," she said.

"I am getting better, you know?" he said, eyes closed against the sun.

"I can see that," she replied, her voice choking up; then she hastily left to put on the coffee.

NOT KNOWING WHETHER what Bullard heard was part of a dream state, as he drifted in and out, he shifted gently. He was cautious about shifting too much because, as Leia had said, any sudden movement could cause a jarring to his spine, and the pain could cripple him. It's not that he was still broken; apparently it was more about how his body wasn't used to movement yet, after being in bed for so long.

She had him doing yoga, for God's sake, though, at first, he had argued. Eventually he'd seen the sense of it and was doing it on a daily basis. For some reason he knew that people in his past would laugh at him, yet he didn't have a problem following her instructions here. She was like a guiding light, and, if she told him to move left, he'd move left. He didn't have any reason for his blind obedience, other than the fact that she had been working very hard for quite some time to help him.

And he saw the change in his body as he'd followed along with her instructions. Also, floundering rudderless in this storm with only the broken parts of his memories, he knew he needed to trust somebody. Whether it was safe to trust her, he couldn't tell, but he also had no reason not to. He shifted on the rocks, slowly sitting up and moving closer to the water, as he tried to look around, tried to find the source of the noises.

He saw no sign of anyone, and he wasn't sure what he heard. He knew some wildlife was on the actual island itself because sometimes she told him about them. He didn't think any big cats were here, but he'd been wrong before. As he studied the area around them, trying not to make it look like he was hunting—a move that came naturally, easily—he thought he saw somebody in the bushes across the way. He let his gaze drift past, before coming back to study the area.

Then he noted a set of eyes studying him. He stared right back and called out, "Hello." Immediately the face disappeared. He frowned at that and heard footsteps behind him, but these he recognized.

"Who are you talking to you?" she asked. "Or have you suddenly become psychic?"

He laughed. "I thought I saw somebody in the bushes." Lifting an arm, he pointed in the general direction.

"Interesting," she murmured. "Nobody has said anything to me about being here."

"Well, I'm probably an anomaly that they're all trying to check out," he said quietly.

"And that's possible." She paused, gazing around the area. "Lots of young women here are looking for a big studly man to protect them."

He snorted at that. "Right. I'm not exactly protector material at the moment."

"But you're a big white man on an island," she said quietly. "Plenty of families have girls who would happily marry you."

"Even though I have no job, don't know if I have any assets, or even if I already have a family?"

"Exactly," she said, as she stepped down onto the rocks and handed him a coffee cup.

"Thank you." He took a sniff of the heady brew. "It's always strong and always perfect."

"It's good coffee," she said, "and simple, which I like. I roast it here, grind it, and make it myself."

"Such a simple life for a woman who isn't simple at all."

"I'm very simple," she said lightly.

He turned to look at her and shook his head. "You're anything but. You're a guardian angel, ... an angel of some kind anyway." She snorted. "You've done an incredible job looking after me."

"I've only done what anybody would do," she said immediately.

"Well, I don't know many people who would have looked after me like this," he said. "I don't even know where or how you found me."

"In the ocean."

Something was in her voice. He turned to look at her. "Do you know what happened?"

"Not for sure," she said. "I wondered ..."

"What is it you wonder?"

She hesitated, and then, as if making a decision, she said, "A plane blew up. I know that people are looking for survivors."

"How long ago?"

"Right at the same time I found you," she said. "Maybe the day before. I'm not sure."

He took a slow deep breath and let it out. "That's a little disconcerting."

"Yes," she said. "It was."

"Did you tell anyone?"

"No," she said, "I didn't."

He stared at her. "Did you have a reason why?"

"Instinct told me not to," she said, with a glare.

He stared straight back at her, as if she were willing him to judge her for making a decision that impacted him, when she had no justifiable reason for going one direction or the other. "*Instinct*," he said, rolling the idea around in his mind. Nothing wrong with that; he just didn't know why.

"Yes," she said. "I felt like you were in danger."

He looked at her in surprise. "The only reason I would be in danger is if I were on that plane, and it was deliberately shot down."

"Exactly," she said. "I know that I have no idea, but still I haven't gone out of my way to tell the authorities you're alive. You had no identification on you. So I don't even know who you are, except that you told me how you thought you were called Bullard."

"Right," he said. "I remember telling you that."

"And that's a very strange name," she said, "but I didn't know if it was your name or somebody else's. So, in theory, I didn't have any reason to take it further."

"Except you said that people could be looking for me," he replied in a neutral voice.

"Yes," she said, "there could be."

"But you didn't want them to find me, right?"

"Only if they are good and not bad people. I wanted the good people to find you," she said, "but not until you were strong enough to handle whatever they would tell you."

He stared out at the beautiful sunlight dappling across the water, thinking how something could be so serene and idyllic, while, at the same time, Leia was afraid it could be a mirage, and someone was trying to get him. He didn't have any reason to doubt her, but he had no reason to believe her either. But something in the background of his brain cells nudged him in that direction. "Now that you have reason to know that I'll make it and that I'm steadily getting stronger," he said, "I need to contact my team."

"You've asked for that several times," she said steadily. "Yet you've never given me any way to actually do it."

He frowned at that. "That does pose a problem, doesn't it?"

"It does because, so far, I don't have anything more than the name *Bullard* to go on."

"Right, and do we have phones?"

"Not necessarily," she said. "Every once in a while somebody from the mainland heads over here. I have no communication here."

He shook his head slowly, amazed. "Do you know how strange that is?"

"I know," she said cheerfully. "But it's a very peaceful way to live."

He studied her for a moment. "That's important to you, isn't it?"

"Yes, and it has been for a very long time," she replied.

"Okay," he said. "So, now that I'm getting better, I need to check in and find out what's going on with my world."

"I was hoping you would find out through your own memories, before somebody came here and shocked you with some unpleasant truths," she murmured.

"But again, that's assuming they are unpleasant. We

don't know that."

"True." But she didn't say anymore.

He couldn't tell much from her tone because it always had that touch of calm serenity. "Do you ever get angry?"

"I hope not. I try not to anymore," she said. "I spent what seemed like years being angry, and I've worked hard at letting that go."

"What happens if you go back to civilization?" he asked.

"I don't know," she said. "Maybe I'll go back to being angry again."

"And that's not what you want, is it?"

"No, it's not," she said.

"I don't suppose you'll tell me what brought you here, will you?"

"Personal disaster," she said quietly. "Profound personal loss gave me a reason to crawl into my skin and to stay there."

"I think I understand that," he said.

"I hope so," she said, "and I hope that my need for privacy is something you also respect." She got up and took his empty coffee cup. "Don't stay out here too long, and, when you're ready to come back, just let me know." And, with that, she turned and walked away.

CHAPTER 3

I T WAS HARD for Leia to keep up a conversation when she knew that something traumatic was about to happen to him. He would leave and leave her here alone, and she had to decide whether she would do anything about it. His wasn't a world she wanted to go back to. In her experience, it was a world filled with pain, loneliness, anger, and injustice. All aspects of life that she had done her best to leave permanently behind.

But he was right in saying that she was hiding. She *was* hiding here when she'd first arrived. The island had welcomed her when they found out she had medical skills, and she'd spent a lot of time helping people manage various conditions and minor ailments. They looked at her with benevolence and generally let her live in peace. But it was definitely a hiding of sorts, and now, all these years later, she had to admit that fear prevented her from moving forward.

It was a beautiful place to live but a very simple existence, though maybe that was okay too. Maybe she could go forward without having to do anything further with her education and her training. She didn't want to retrain, and she highly doubted the last several years would be counted as additional medical experience for her. But it certainly had helped her get her head together.

She just didn't know what to think about Bullard and

then his comment about somebody in the bushes. She put away the coffee cups, put on her sandals, and changed direction, coming up to where Bullard had said someone had been watching. She also understood his confusion because he'd had so many nightmares, even wide awake, where he couldn't see that the monsters were in his dreams. They were his history, and it had taken her a lot of time and effort to calm him down and for him to see the difference.

Even now she wasn't sure if she believed him about being watched. But, as she wandered around to the far side where such a person would have been, she frowned at the sight of footprints in the sand. Clearly they had stood here for a while, shuffling their feet, churning up the sand as they watched Bullard. And that just creeped her out and changed the atmosphere entirely. Something about the peacefulness of the island was changing. And maybe not for the better.

"Anybody there?" Bullard called out to her.

Startled, she peered through the bushes at him. "No," she said. "I found footprints though, so somebody was here."

"I saw them then," he said, satisfied.

She just smiled. Sitting off to the side, he was still pale and too lean for a man of his size and stature. But now he was gaining weight every day and beginning to use his wasting muscles. She was amazed at what a vibrant man he was and didn't dare envision what he must have been like in his prime. Truly charismatic and larger-than-life in every way. She stepped down toward the pool. "Are you still doing okay over there?"

"Better than I expected actually," he said, and he gestured to the surroundings. "This is amazing, and I can feel myself getting stronger, as I soak it all in."

She nodded. "Agreed, but I don't want you to overdo

it."

"I will overdo it," he said on a chuckle. "Just because I can."

Then she watched his countenance change completely, like a dark cloud blocking the sunlight. "How much of an issue is the person who was over there?"

"Normally I would say not much," she said. "Some of the islanders are curious about you, or maybe they're just trying to see how you are doing. And I wasn't kidding about the women."

"Maybe," he said. "Or maybe it's something else entirely."

She walked over to the water's edge, then hopped across several of the rocks, navigating her way across the water toward where he sat. Wearing one of the long flowing dresses she preferred on the island, she held her skirts up, until she finally made it across and landed nearby. "Do you think somebody's after you?" she asked, looking directly at him.

"I think it's a possibility," he said. "How could it not be, given what you know?"

"It's not what I know," she said quietly, "as much as what I've heard." She sat down beside him. "I don't know for sure that you are in danger."

"But you're thinking that we are," he said.

"We? No," she said, shaking her head at the thought. "You."

"Sweetie," he said. "You're the one who's kept me safe, and that means you're in danger too." She stared at him in shock. "Had you not considered that?"

"No, of course not." Yet, after she thought about it for a moment, she shrugged. "And it doesn't matter in the end, because I wouldn't have done anything differently."

"Exactly," he said, "that's because of who you are."

She looked at him, then smiled. "I'm just me."

"Yep. An angel in disguise," he said, returning her smile.

She rolled her eyes at that, then noticed the sun beating down on his shoulders, already turning pinkish. "You need to move into the shade at least or back to bed. You must be worn out by now."

"Yeah, I am, and back to bed is what I need to do," he said, "but it's hard to leave this place. It's so amazing out here, so beautiful and serene that I just want to stay out here."

"You can come back later on tonight or tomorrow morning," she said.

"I hope so," he said, and, with her assistance, he got to his feet and grabbed his crutches. Slowly they walked back to the hut that he called his own. It wasn't much more than a rough platform, a simple padding for a bed, and some netting above. He stood there for a long moment, looking at her. "I don't know how I came to be here really," he said, "but I am delighted that you found me."

"I am too." She smiled.

"Did I ever say, *Thank you?*"

"*Hmm*, I don't know that you did," she said, "but that isn't necessary."

"Maybe not," he replied, "but it does feel like I need to acknowledge the fact that you kept me alive all this time, when a lot of other people would have turned me over to somebody else or wouldn't have gotten involved at all."

"You're just lucky that I had the training to fix you up."

"That's another thing," he said. "You have advanced medical training, don't you?"

"I do," she said.

"And yet you're out here," he said, the unspoken question lingering in the air.

"That world is over for me."

"Does it have to be?" he asked.

"I wouldn't say that it *has* to be," she said, "but it's that way because I choose it to be so." And, with that, it was clear she wouldn't say any more.

With a nod, he said, "Okay. You're entitled to your secrets, but, anytime you want to share, I'm happy to listen."

She looked up at him. "Maybe I'll share more of mine when you discover yours and get them out in the open."

"I wonder if that will ever happen?" he said. "Sometimes it feels like my brain will never work right and won't let me put all these random pieces together."

"It will," she said. "Just maybe not today."

At that, he hobbled around and got settled on his bed, suddenly looking weary. He was asleep almost instantly.

LEIA LEFT BULLARD to return to where she had seen the footprints. It bothered her to realize someone had been watching Bullard. If it was anybody from the island who knew her, they would have come and said something. They hadn't made the visit seem more sinister, and she didn't like that at all. There was no need for it, but, despite a thorough study of the site, she couldn't find anything to identify who it may have been. She then made the quick trip across the island, hoping that Bullard would sleep long enough.

The old medicine woman looked up at Leia with a smile when she arrived. "Good," she said. "Terk left another message."

"And what is it this time?" Leia asked, looking sideways

at the seer, not wanting to hear the message.

"He said, *He's coming.*"

At that, her breath was gone, and it was a moment before she could breathe again. Slowly she nodded and took a deep breath.

"Good, you understand," the medicine woman said. "How is he?"

"He's getting much better."

"But not good enough yet, is he?"

"No," she said. "He's also not sure what's going on."

"We'll have to find out," the old woman said.

"It'll be the outsiders."

"Yes, it will. Like it or not, change is coming. Danger is coming," the old woman said.

"I'm not ready for change," Leia said.

"I know, and that's too bad because it's happening anyway."

Leia nodded slowly, knowing that the old woman knew things that Leia did not. Finally, when no other messages came to the old woman, Leia turned and headed back, moving quickly toward the hut where Bullard slept. If nothing else, she needed to get him as strong as possible before things changed. She knew that whatever was coming would bring an element of danger, and neither of them were prepared for it.

No way they were even slightly prepared for the kind of danger she suspected that Bullard might be used to. And despite his rapidly improving physical condition, they still needed several more weeks. She could only hope they got them.

When she got home, she made a note on her calendar of the old woman's words regarding Bullard's progress and kept a careful watch for another full week. There were no incidents, no further sightings of strangers in the brush. She felt like they were waiting, and something intense was going on in the background. It was almost as if Bullard realized that things had shifted because every day now he was doing exercises to build back some muscle. He was walking more, doing push-ups, also some kind of martial arts that she didn't recognize.

Never asking him about it, she sat quietly, watching him go through the disciplined motions. What began as stilted awkward movements had transformed over ten days and now resembled something more like velvet in motion. She smiled when he finally stopped, the sweat on his skin now thick and glistening in the sun. "Ready for a swim?"

Straightening, he looked at her, still breathing hard as he nodded. "Absolutely." He looked at the crutches and looked at her. The worn-out splint had fallen away, and he was now on his own. "Do you think we're good without that?"

"Why don't we go find out?" she said. She hopped up and grabbed several towels.

He looked at her, puzzled, and said, "Don't you need to get on a bathing suit?"

"I have one on," she said, with a laugh, then led the way to the pool. At the water, she carefully dropped her dress of the day. She had ten of them in a variety of bright fabrics that she rotated. She washed them in the water when she bathed, and let them dry in the air. Today's selection was a deep fuchsia with purple accents and bright yellow flowers. She had only walked down a few steps when she felt an odd gaze. Turning, she looked at Bullard. "What?"

He shook his head. "I think this is the first time I've seen you swimming. At least close up."

"Does that mean you've been watching me from a distance?" she teased.

He grinned and said, "You are dynamite, so anybody would take notice."

"Well, if it helps you heal, go ahead and look," she said, with a laugh, then stepped into the water and let her body sink under the waves. The water was moving beautifully today. The waves were backing out from the collision that occurred where the river poured into the ocean. It was truly a wondrous experience, and she floated, letting her body relax and let go of the stress she had felt ever since hearing the latest words from the medicine woman.

Knowing that this peace would come to an end, she'd felt herself tense, uneasy, waiting for an attack. Yet she had no justification for it and no reason to suspect such an attack, except that it was out there and that it wasn't going away.

When she heard a heavy splash, and her body roiled from the waves Bullard created, she smiled to see him pop up in the water beside her.

"It's hard to float out here," he said. "It's a lot rougher where the river pours into the ocean."

"That is true," she said, "but it also helps you train. Look over here." She pointed. "If you stick close to these rocks, there is almost no current."

Nodding, he grabbed onto a rock and said, "There was a hard rain as well, and I gather it has quite an effect here."

"It also depends on the tide," she said, "and today the ocean is just rough." They stayed out here, floating and swimming until they were tired, then got out to sit on the rocky ledge.

"How long will you hide here?" he asked, then he

winced. "I'm sorry. That wasn't exactly the best way to say it."

"I came here to hide," she said, "but I don't know that I'm still hiding."

"But you're not back to normal life."

"No," she said, "I'm not. But I'm not sure how much of that is because I'm still hiding or if I've just not gotten around to changing it."

"It's really gorgeous here," he said, "and I can see being here for a holiday, but I'm not sure how I would feel living here full-time."

She wondered at that. "I guess that's true. But I came here for a very different reason, and my recovery, although slow, is definitely completed."

"And you still won't tell me why?" he asked.

"I don't think it's important," she said.

"Maybe not," he said. "Unless whoever is hiding in the bushes all the time is here because of you."

She turned to look at him, suddenly pale. "Have you seen him again?"

"Every couple days," he said. "One of these days I'll be strong enough to drag him out and find out what the hell he's up to."

She frowned at that. "I did talk to several people on the island, and nobody knows who would do that."

"Well, the other thing to consider is the fact that you're a stunningly beautiful woman, and you live here alone."

"Yes," she said, "there is that, and thank you for the compliment, but I don't really see that it's made any difference. I've been here for years alone, and the islanders know me well."

"Maybe this isn't someone from the island," he said.

"And that's possible." She pondered the idea, then shook her head. "I still don't see why though."

"Maybe we're not supposed to know the why of everything," he said, "but there's been a definite change in the atmosphere."

"I've felt it." She sighed. "And I was looking for a way to change it back."

"That won't happen," he said. "Whatever's happening in the outside world has arrived here."

"But is it because of you or because of me?" she asked.

"It could be both," he said, with a shrug. "One of the difficulties in any of our missions is finding out what truly is going on behind something like this."

Missions? She looked at him, her mouth open in surprise. "You've remembered?"

He gave her a gentle smile. "I've remembered a lot of it, yes."

Squaring her shoulders, she took a deep breath, exhaling slowly. "So, is it good or bad?"

"It's both," he said.

"When are you leaving?" she asked, taking another deep breath.

"I'm not sure, but it needs to be soon."

"Why?"

"Because I can't be sure that whoever blew my plane out of the air won't come here after you."

"Why me?" she asked.

"Because you've been looking after me," he said. "The men I hunt in this world are ugly, and they won't rest until they know for sure I'm gone."

"And if you're not gone?"

"They'll do their best to make sure I am," he said.

"Great. So violence is on the way to my sanctuary, huh?"

"But you already knew that," he said.

"I suspected as much and have been waiting for that kind of a change. But I was hoping I was wrong."

"You're not wrong," he said. "So the sooner I can get out of here, the better."

"Do you want to contact your team?"

"Yes, so how will I do that from here?"

"Not easily," she noted, "but I might get a cell phone."

Looking at her, he said, "I know you don't want that kind of intrusion here, but the sooner I can contact my team, the sooner I'll be out of your hair."

Instantly she felt a cold chill rippling down her spine. "It will be very strange," she said, her voice smooth and even, as always.

"In what way?"

"You've been a big part of my life for a long time now."

"True," he said, "and, for that, I am very sorry."

"I'm not," she said, with the gentlest of smiles.

"Because you didn't mind having somebody to look after or because it gave you a purpose?"

His insight had her staring at him. "I don't know," she said. "When you're hurting, you run away and hide. But it's hard to know when that hurt has stopped and when you're actually okay, versus being stuck and still hiding."

"That's why I was asking if you saw yourself leaving."

"*Hmm*," she said. "Maybe. But I don't know where I would go. This has been my home for many years now."

"And it's still a place to come back to," he said. "It's so beautiful, and I'll always have great memories of it."

"But you're leaving, so it won't be the same," she said.

He looked at her, then hesitated and said, "Leia, come

with me."

She stared at him in surprise.

"Don't tell me that you haven't thought about it," he said, an awkwardness evident in his voice.

She studied him for a long moment. "Depending on what you mean," she said, "I've often wondered about leaving, but I always had this immediate negative response."

Nodding, he stared out at the world around them. "Right," he said. "I guess I was hoping for a little more than that." He got up slowly, wincing as he did so.

"You're not ready to leave," she said, jumping to her feet.

"Maybe not," he said, "but there isn't exactly time right now."

"Have you got all your memories back?"

"No," he said. "I'm not sure on some things yet. That's another reason to connect with my team, to see how many holes they can fill in."

"Do you remember your team?"

"Some of them," he said, frowning. "And some of it is still a blank."

"Are you sure it's safe to contact them?"

"I don't know who else I'd contact," he said. "They are men I would trust with my life."

"Well, that's what you'd be trusting them with," she said gently. "If you think about it, that's exactly what you'd be doing."

"Only if they had something to do with that plane crash. Which I don't even know for sure was sabotage."

"True." She nodded. Hopping from the rock, she grabbed her dress and went to put it over her swimsuit.

"Don't."

"Don't what?"

"Don't hide all that beauty," he said. His gaze was intense, and she felt herself flushing hot and cold. An attraction had been growing between them, but she hadn't thought he'd even known what it was. She'd thought he hadn't been well enough to know, but now he was like an animal in his prime, gaining strength every day, so she wasn't surprised that this would rear its head. She nodded with a smile and said, "I have often been without my dress."

"I'm not sure about that," he said. "It seems that you wear it almost as a uniform."

She was unoffended at his directness. "It's not so much a uniform as a defense system."

Immediately he frowned. "Did somebody hurt you?" His voice was harsh, and he was clearly agitated.

"Well, I was definitely hurt, but, if you mean attacked or raped, the answer is no."

"Good," he said, calmer already. "I would want that man's name and would make sure that he paid."

She looked at him in surprise. "Would you do that?"

He frowned at her response. "Absolutely. I recognize the value of an angel, even if someone else doesn't."

CHAPTER 4

BULLARD MEANT EVERY word. The last thing he would allow in this world were people who tried to damage the angels, and abusing a woman was not something Bullard could tolerate. He may not have full recollection of his history or who he was even now, but he knew who he was on the inside. He studied Leia, knowing she had secrets that he had yet to delve into. He didn't want to push, but, now that he felt better, her history and everything else about her was on his mind. Matter of fact, she was constantly on his mind, not to mention under his skin and in his heart. He didn't have a clue who and what she was outside of this place, but he knew he needed to find out. "Will you ever tell me what's going on in your world?"

"Maybe," she said gently. "But it's hardly today's issue."

"That depends on whether whoever is out there watching us is a part of it."

"No," she said, with a shake of her head. "Definitely not."

"I'm not so sure about that."

"I think you like to have answers with the *T*s crossed and the *I*s dotted," she murmured.

He looked at her, nodded. "You know what? I think you're probably right about that. But is that wrong?"

"No," she said, "but justice doesn't always come with the

answers we want, does it?"

Again that question in her statement made him wonder about her history. "May I come up to your place?"

She looked at him in surprise. "If you mean my cabin, yes, of course. That's where I cook, so, if you want, we could have dinner up there tonight."

He raised his eyebrows. "Is that like a date?"

She chuckled. "You'd have to be pretty desperate to call that a date."

"Hey, special times," he said, looking around him. "Many people would pay millions of dollars to come to a place like this and to enjoy everything all this has to offer."

"Maybe," she said, "but that doesn't mean it's the right thing to do."

Again, an interesting statement from her. He just nodded and smiled.

"Besides, we don't want millions of people coming here," she said. "I'm here for the peace and quiet."

"Peace and quiet was what you came for," he said, "but you stayed because it was easy." She looked at him in surprise, but he gave her a knowing nod. "Believe me. As I slowly regain everything in my mind, I understand completely."

"Maybe," she said, "but until you walk a mile …"

"I get it, and you're entitled to have privacy."

"Glad to hear you say that," she said, "because I was getting the feeling you'll be up in my business, trying to get answers all the time." He gave her that lopsided grin, and she continued, "I can't imagine anybody cares enough about me after all this time to be hiding in the bushes."

"You're a delightful person, Leia. You're a beautiful woman in her prime, so I'm sure many men would like to have you walk beside them."

"If you really mean have sex with me," she said candidly, "I've had a few offers, but nothing I cared to respond to."

He'd stared at her in surprise. "Is there a reason why not?"

"Of course there is," she said but refused further comment.

He frowned at that because it was just one more in a series of mysteries, and he didn't need that. He was looking for answers. Something solid that would make him feel like they were getting somewhere. But she also wouldn't let him get away with that. She was a very private woman in many ways. Yet open in others. She was also very skilled, yet kept herself isolated. He couldn't understand the contrast and wondered again what had happened to her.

"Come up to my place when you feel better," she said. And, with that, she stepped away from the water and headed to her cabin.

He watched her go, and, seeing the gentle sway of her hips, he realized he was obviously healing because his whole body responded to every ounce of her. She was sleek, smooth, and honey-toned from so much sun, not to mention gorgeous inside and out, plus incredibly kind and generous. She had been the saving grace in the craziness of his world. He owed her so much, yet knew she would be offended if he even brought up repaying her. Hell, he probably would be too, if their situations were reversed.

At the same time, he couldn't quite let go of the pain at the prospect of leaving her. He sat once more on the rock ledge around the ponds. That brought on his tentative questions about her interest in leaving. Not that she had given a very solid answer, but still it was something. He just couldn't imagine not having her around him. He'd been here for what seemed like forever now, but he understood it was only a matter of months. That thought turned his mind back to wondering what the hell had happened in his world and who would know. To try and get answers, she said she could get him a cell phone. Well, he needed that, and he needed it now.

The longer Bullard sat here thinking about it, the more irritated he got because he wanted a cell phone in his hands right this instant. But island life didn't work that way. It was very much a case of tomorrow—or whenever even. Nobody seemed to give a crap about timing or who would need something today, not next week. He couldn't imagine how long it had taken Leia to adjust to this world, but she had.

He also understood that she was the one who had stitched his head and elsewhere, but he didn't know what else she might have done. She had looked after him like a baby for weeks. He felt no shame in that because he'd been terribly injured. And, at the same time, he had looked after many a person in the same way. But now that he was healthier, he felt a restlessness taking over. He gazed about, wondering at such a gorgeous location.

In the western world, this would have been eaten up by a millionaire as a place of their own, locked down so nobody could come in and enjoy it. But, if it were a public park, he could just imagine how badly it would be abused by people who wouldn't take proper care of it. That mindless devastation of Mother Nature also hurt him. Somewhere along the line, he'd apparently picked up quite a critical view of the world around him. It might be justified, or maybe not, but it's the one he carried, so he could only assume that enough had been going on in his world to give him that kind of an attitude. As soon as he thought about that, more memories slipped into his mind.

He sat here for a long moment as he took a trip down memory lane, revisiting old missions, even throughout the United States. With friends. Some names were still elusive, as were the people behind them. He got a sense of Levi and knew that he was important, but Bullard didn't understand quite how or why he couldn't pick up the names of different members of his team. He remembered Ryland and Kano and Garret and Cain. Bullard frowned as he thought about them, wishing the entire set of memories would slide back.

At the moment, those memories were stuck in limbo, as if looking for that extra little prod to open them up. It was frustrating in many ways, but Bullard had come a long way since he'd first started this recall of his memories, so it was hard to imagine that it would stop now. He just didn't want to even be concerned about it. And yet he was concerned because that's just the way life worked. At the same time he had to let his body—and his mind—heal a little more.

He still had time before dinner, so he put himself through a punishing set of push-ups and sit-ups, trying to get his muscles to respond the way they needed to. He knew he'd always been in tip-top physical form and also knew that he was still a ways away from that.

Closing his eyes, he let his body slide into a series of moves that were instinctive and likely as old as he was. It was a mixture, a combination of martial arts, yoga, and tai chi; yet he immediately knew it was toning his body and toning his mind, as he prepared for his return to the world. He'd been gone just long enough that, if his accident had been no accident, some people would be very unhappy to see him again.

He also knew others would be completely overwhelmed because he had survived. As he had that thought, he suddenly realized with joy that Ice would be one of them. Ice and Levi. Then there was Izzie. He frowned for a moment, wondering at the name, until Isabella's face came into his mind, and he realized it was his niece. He smiled at the thought. Cranky, cantankerous, difficult Izzie.

And yet she was the only blood relative in his life. Blachard was a half brother, as they shared a father, and Bullard had always considered Izzie family. He gave a happy sigh at the memory and the joy at having her firmly back in his mind. Now that he could let her know he was okay, and he assumed the team would have contacted her about the accident. But then again, if his flight had been sabotaged, had his team been targeted too? Had they been attacked?

Had somebody gone after everyone? He had run a big successful security-related business that had interfered in takeovers, coups, high-level crime, and espionage. His company was an international asset that had made a lot of enemies. He always knew there was a chance of somebody coming back after him; it was a dangerous life that way. But he'd hoped that he would have had some hint as to what was going on before now.

Just then he heard Leia call out that dinner was ready. He looked up, lifted a hand, and carefully moved from the river toward her place. He was interested to see just what a meal at her place meant. Somehow he had to get her to relax enough around him to make some progress in getting to know her. Not that she was nervous, just that she wasn't used to sharing her island.

She'd spent so many years hidden away here that either she had become somebody who preferred her own space with her own silence and didn't really know how to share herself anymore, or she was worried that he would say or do something that could set off feelings that she didn't want to deal with. All in all, it was a very strange way to wake up to the world. And *wake up* was exactly what he had done. Every moment, every hour, more and more memories flooded back, and he couldn't wait to fill in the rest of the holes.

CHAPTER 5

S EVERAL DAYS LATER Leia realized just how strong Bullard really was getting, as she looked up at him, using a low-lying branch as a pull-up bar. Slow and steady, he'd been working at it every day. He wasn't yet in what she envisioned as his top form, but he was about 80 percent there. And she knew that the probing questions and pushing wouldn't stop. Now that he was almost free and he felt it physically, he was pushing himself hard. All he could talk about at this point was getting back to the world he had left behind and picking up the pieces of a life that she could only imagine.

He stepped out into the water after his push-ups and then went back at it again, jumping up lightly. He stretched and twisted in the early morning sun, as she came down with a cup of coffee for him. He looked up, then smiled. "I can't believe how good I feel."

"That's great," she said, trying hard to insert a note of joviality into her voice. But it was hard because, as soon as he felt good enough, he'd be gone, and she wasn't ready for that. The minute that happened, she knew this place—that was home to her—would feel incredibly lonely, and she wasn't sure how she would handle it. Of course she had been through enough in her life to know that she could handle him leaving; she didn't get a choice after all. But, at the same time, it was something she really wasn't looking forward to. Shaking off her sadness, she asked, "Ready for coffee?"

"I am," he replied. Accepting the cup from her hand, he turned to look around and said, "I'll really miss this place."

She nodded but didn't say anything. What could she say? "When are you leaving?" The words tumbled out without her getting a chance to control them.

He turned to look back at her. "Did you get me a cell phone?"

"No, but I've asked for one though. They're heading to the mainland today, so, with any luck, maybe tonight."

He nodded slowly. "Does anything here happen fast?"

Her eyes twinkled at that. "Island living," she said, "so the answer is no."

"It really is an island life, isn't it?"

She nodded. "It's a special way to live."

"I don't think I've ever really experienced it before," he said, marveling at it. "I feel I've been on that *go, go, go* life since forever."

"Exactly," she said. "And, once you have, it's pretty hard to let go of."

"That brings us back to my question. What will you do?"

"Nothing here has changed for me," she said. "You'll leave and go back to the world you know, and I'll be here, living my life, like I always do," she said simply.

"Won't you be lonely?"

"Meaning that I won't survive without you around?" she said, her grin widening.

He laughed. "Okay, I guess that's kind of foolish of me, isn't it? But you've become a major part of my world for the last few months. It will feel very strange to just leave you behind."

"Well, I don't imagine there's a place for me in your world," she said. "It doesn't sound like you were short on any kind of attention. Besides, for all you know, you have a wife and four kids at home." She had said it lightly, but her gaze searched his face.

He shook his head. "No. None of that for me and my memories are filling in rapidly."

She was happy for him because it was hard to imagine what life would be like if you were constantly missing a big chunk of who you were.

"No wife," he said easily. "Although I'm still not sure about a couple people. They—it's just that I don't really have explanations for how much in my life they are, how it all fits."

"Is that Ice?"

He nodded. "She's married to a good friend of mine," he said.

Leia stared at him in surprise. "Oh."

He nodded. "See? So I'm not sure what that's all about."

"It'll fill in slowly. Just let it happen in its own time," she urged. Inside, her own heart was lightening. Maybe he was pining for someone after all. It didn't seem possible, considering how big and strong and virile this man was. But still, she was happy to know that no family waited for him. That didn't sound quite right because, of course, she wanted to know that he was happy and surrounded by people who loved him. But that was a long way from having a partner, staring at the door, wondering if he'd ever come home again.

"I have to leave soon," he said.

"I get that," she said. "So hopefully the cell phone is coming tonight."

"We've been watched."

She looked at him in surprise. "What? We knew about the one person for several days, but I haven't seen anything since. Have you?"

"Not the same person. No," he said. "But I have seen others."

"Strangers?" she asked, stiffening.

He looked at her in surprise. "I don't know if they're strangers to you or not," he said. "This is your life and your friends here. But they are strangers to me."

She nodded. "Which doesn't necessarily mean anything."

"One appeared to be a soldier of some kind," he said. "He was very quiet and stealthy, moving through the area. He certainly didn't want to be seen."

"Did you talk to him?"

"No," he said, with that lopsided grin that she'd come to love. "Absolutely not."

"And why is that?"

"Because I got the feeling he was after more than conversation."

She stared at him for a long moment, studying the hardness in his gaze. "Maybe," she said, "but maybe you're just overreacting."

He looked at her and said, "Sweetheart, overreacting keeps me alive."

"And are you so sure that he's after you? That you need to be worried about it?"

"Without a doubt."

"Then you did right," she said simply.

He frowned. "Is it all that simple?"

"Sometimes the only thing we can do," she said, "is follow our heart."

"Well, I don't have anybody in my past pulling my heart one way or the other," he said. "What about you?"

"Nope," she said.

"Ever married?"

"Nope."

He looked at her in surprise. "You're wasting the best years of your life here on the island alone," he said. "I'm not trying to insult you, but it makes me sad."

"Maybe I've had enough of people," she replied. With that, she turned and walked up several of the rock ledges from the river. "I'm not sure I can leave this place anymore."

"Sure you can. You don't have to leave it permanently."

"No," she said, "that's true. This is my space, my corner of the island."

"You own the land?"

"Yes," she said, "I do."

"So you really could leave and come back anytime you wanted to," he said.

"I'd probably get to the edge of my property and decide that was far enough," she said, laughing. He didn't say anything more. She wasn't sure what else to say, so she turned to practical matters. "If you're ready for breakfast, I have some fresh buns."

"You don't buy much for supplies here, do you?"

"Only in the last few months," she said.

He looked around and nodded. "Yeah, speaking of that, I need to make that right, so what do I—" At that she turned and glared at him fiercely, and he held up a hand. "I'm just asking."

"No. You don't owe me anything," she said. "Pay it forward when you see someone needing a hand."

"That's easy," he said. "I'm pretty sure I do it all the time anyway."

"Do you?"

"I think so," he said, frowning. "But you've got me there because that memory isn't quite filling in."

"What if you find out that you're not who you think you are?" she asked.

"I'm pretty sure I know who I am at this point," he said. "I've got enough memories in there that, although the spotty holes are very frustrating, a lot of them are mostly filled in to understand the kind of work I did, which side of the fence I worked on, and the type of skills I had." He looked down at his body and said, "By the way, I've done a hell of a lot of medical work."

She looked at him in surprise. "Are you sure?"

"Yeah, so if you were in the same condition I was when you found me, I could have done the same for you."

"You're a doctor?"

"I think so," he said, frowning, "but I'm not exactly sure. I have the training and experience, but I don't know if I have the certificates."

"Military doctor maybe?" she asked.

"Who knows? Maybe," he said thoughtfully. "But I have done a lot of surgeries. And, at home, I have extremely high-end equipment."

She looked at him with interest. "Knowing that," she said, "is worth its weight in gold."

"It is, and I think a whole community depends on me." He again frowned at that. "That sounds very arrogant of me, and I don't mean it that way."

"So you have like a surgery day or an open clinic maybe?"

His face cleared, and he nodded. "All the neighbors in the surrounding community," he said, "they come to me."

"And you live where?"

"Africa," he said, triumphant, since that had been a gap that was problematic. Then he stopped and said, "Something about Tunisia too. On the border?" He shook his head. "I don't know, but I know my world is pretty global."

"Must be nice," she said, and she proceeded to prepare breakfast, while trying to keep her thoughts to herself.

"You'll be okay when I leave?" he asked again.

She looked at him in surprise. "I was okay before you got here. Why wouldn't I be when you go?"

"You didn't have people skulking around in the bushes before, for one thing."

"That's very true," she said. "At least none that I saw. Obviously having you here has created some interest. Most of the people don't know too much about it. The local villagers did, but you were close to dying at that point in time. I don't think they thought you would live, so now that you're up and about, you're causing more of a stir."

"But who would have seen me?"

"Fishermen for one," she said. "And that's an easy thing for them to see while they're out there." She pointed toward the ocean.

"I guess," he said doubtfully.

"And maybe somebody contacted the village, asking about you," she said. "We're not that isolated. We try to stick to ourselves and away from the big bad world out there, but we're not completely isolated."

"Are you the only one from the outside world who lives here?"

"Pretty much," she said. "Most of the others are locals,

who have lived here all their lives, which is why you're an anomaly."

"Yep, but that's okay. I'm used to standing out and attracting attention," he said. "So will you ever go back and fight whatever injustice happened in your world?"

"No," Leia replied, frowning. "Some things you just can't fight."

"Or maybe you have to change the way the war is won," he said.

"There are always people more powerful than you who do whatever they can to make you the bad guy instead of taking the blame themselves," she said. "Honestly I don't think I even care anymore."

"What if somebody else cared for you?"

She looked at him and said, "You can't fight everybody's battles. You need to go get your own life back together first."

"Hey, my life has been running smoothly in my absence."

He said this with such a note of authority that she had to laugh. "Seriously?"

"Absolutely," he said.

"Well, it would be nice if your team is that good," she said, "but I wouldn't count on it."

"I can definitely count on it," he said. "They are that good, without a doubt."

She stared at him. "Then they are better than everybody else I know."

"They are," he said, "and I won't hide that fact. Because part of the reason they are so good is because they are my team. Chosen, trained, and looked after by me."

She studied him for the longest time, seeing the pride, the joy on his face and realizing just how far removed his world was from hers. She looked around at the island, sensing change, much like the tsunami that she'd already felt coming toward her, but she wasn't ready for it now any more than she had been prepared back then. "I get it," she said and then motioned at the fresh buns in front of him. "You better eat."

"And if I don't?" he asked, sitting down and looking up at her. "Oh, is there any more coffee, by chance?"

She smiled and said, "If you don't eat the bun, I'll eat it for you. And, yes, there's plenty of coffee." She walked over and poured him a cup, before sitting down across from him. She picked out one of the four rolls and gently buttered it, before taking a small bite herself.

"You don't eat much, do you?" he asked.

"I don't need to eat much," she said. "I spend my days here in peaceful contemplation."

"You were doing some writing as well, I noticed."

"I was," she said. "It's a way to keep my sanity some-times."

"You never told me what you did in the big bad world before you wound up here."

She smiled. "I was a heart surgeon."

He stopped and stared. "Seriously?"

She gave him a sideways look. "Why? Can't women be surgeons in your world?"

He continued to stare at her, looking even more shocked at that. "Of course they can. Some of the best surgeons I know are women," he said, "but what on earth would take you from there to here?"

"Sometimes life doesn't go the way we thought it would go," she said, clearly uncomfortable with the attention.

"If you tell me that you threw it all away for some asshole of a man, I'll get really angry."

She laughed at that. "Well, let's just say an asshole of a man was part of the reason, but it certainly wasn't a love affair gone wrong."

"Okay, now I want the details," he snapped.

"You can want all you like," she said. "That doesn't mean I'm giving them to you."

He glared at her in frustration, while she remained serene. "I can't understand how you can live here so calm and peaceful if something bad happened to you."

"But that's exactly why I am here," she said. "Not all injustices get resolved the way we want them to."

"That doesn't mean we have to let it all go either," he growled, clearly upset.

"You're really pretty much black-and-white, aren't you?"

"I don't like to see the people I care about getting hurt."

"Neither do I," she said. "Sometimes we make the wrong decisions, and sometimes people go against us regardless."

"Could I please have an explanation?"

"Not really anything to say." But she considered it, and, just as she would open up and share something with him, a noise came from around the corner of her cabin. She got up and walked over there, ever mindful of his comment about somebody watching them. As she got to the corner, Paolo emerged, smiling broadly with the typical island friendliness.

"I brought you fish," he said, holding out his hand. She accepted them. "It looks lovely, thank you," she said warmly.

"Your patient, how is he doing?" Paolo asked.

"Much better," she said, and, at that, she turned to see Bullard stepping away from her cabin.

Paolo's gaze widened at the size of him. "Wow, he's doing much better."

Bullard smiled and said, "I'm almost healed. Did you bring a cell phone?"

He frowned and looked at him. "I forgot." He turned to look behind him. "My brother went though. Let me see if I can get one from him." With that, he turned and disappeared.

"He forgot?" Bullard said, his voice a low growl.

"He doesn't lie," she said, turning back to him. She thought she heard another sound around the corner. She stepped around the side of the cabin and stared into the trees.

Bullard reached out and put a hand on her shoulder and said, "Remember. We're being watched."

She tensed immediately. "I wasn't expecting to find danger when you got back on your feet," she muttered. "It's a foreign feeling for me."

"No," he said, "you were dealing with the same type of attack. It's just that yours was verbal, whereas mine will be physical."

"Interesting observation," she said. "How did you know?"

"Because if somebody didn't physically beat you, they beat you in other ways."

"Oh, I was definitely hurting," she said. "And I've had no contact from the outer world ever since."

"You just up and left?"

"I did," she said, and, thinking back, she realized how much she had needed that to happen. "When you're hurt, sometimes it's all you can do."

"Absolutely, but, at the same time, you're hiding," he said, "and you have to be prepared to reenter the world at some point. I can't imagine anybody driven enough to become a heart surgeon could be happy here indefinitely."

"Well, I was," she said. "Until a stranger washed up on my boat."

"Is that why you haven't been fishing lately?"

"I've been looking after you," she said, "and Paolo, well, he likes me, so he tends to bring me fish."

Bullard growled behind her back. "That's nice," he said. "As long as he doesn't have any expectations."

"He's male," she said. "Don't you all have expectations?"

He frowned at that and then nodded. "You're right. I guess I have expectations too."

She spun and looked up at him. "And just what are those?"

BULLARD GLARED AT Leia. "Obviously not what you're thinking," he said, "but I would like to not lose you right now."

"Once you go back to your real world," she said, "I'll be a blip on your radar. Just something that happened, and, sure, you'll remember, but soon it'll be a distant memory."

"I don't want you to be a distant memory," he said roughly.

"That's what you say right now," she said, "but, once you get back to that world, it will be completely different."

"Maybe," he said, "but that doesn't mean there isn't room for you in it."

"I'm not sure there is though," she said, "because I don't know that I could handle it."

"If you want to get back to your medicine," he said, "I do have a full-on clinic, with all the equipment you could ever want."

She frowned. "But I'm not licensed to practice in Africa."

"And I'm sure we could make that happen, if you wanted it to."

"I'm not sure I do," she said. "That was part of the world I walked away from."

"But you don't have to keep walking away from it."

"Maybe," she said, "but I'm not sure I'm ready for that kind of change." He frowned. "No," she said. "Listen. My reasons are sound, and I'm just not sure I want to give people a chance to get back at me again."

"All you're doing is making it so I'll have no choice but to look into what happened to you," he said. "It'd be easier if you just told me."

"Maybe, but I don't know that I want to," she said, pulling away from him. "I'm going for a walk. Please don't follow me." With that, she turned and walked away from him.

He stared after her in frustration, trying to figure out what had happened to her. The thought that her medical skills weren't being utilized horrified him, since he came from a world where there were not nearly enough people with those skills. Those they had were worth their weight in gold. He knew people changed careers all the time, finding they didn't have the temperament for the type of work they were doing or something else, but, in her case, she had been hurt. He just didn't know why.

Just then Paolo returned, walking up and handing over a cell phone. He smiled at the newcomer, and Paolo said, "He had it. I had asked him to get it, but I didn't ask him if he'd gotten it before I brought the fish." He shrugged, then, with a big grin and a wave of his hand, he disappeared into the trees.

Bullard wondered how that worked. Was it all so nice and simple here on the island? Were people really that trusting? Part of him looked at the phone, wondering if it was being tracked. Were they that sensitive to life? Did they understand what was going on in the greater world, or were they innocent of the ways of deceit? Then again, they weren't innocent to the ways of money because that's what made the world go around. They may not have the same need for it that other people did, but most cultures didn't turn down money when it was offered.

And people would pay if Paolo had something they wanted, such as knowledge of Bullard's whereabouts. That could be both good and bad because his own team was likely looking for him as well. At least he sure as hell hoped so. He had to hold on to the faith that what was happening was the fight between good and evil, and, as always, he would win that war. It was pretty damn hard to even consider that it wasn't an option.

He looked again at the cell phone, but his instincts prodded him to quickly take off the back and to look for anything added to it. But, no, it was all clear. He sighed with relief at that. He sat down and noted it had a battery, with prepaid minutes. He didn't have a clue how many he had or what the charges would be. He also didn't know how a cell package out here worked or even where the service came from. Thailand maybe. Thinking about the various phone numbers he could call, and knowing that it was important to calculate in time zones, he sat here for a long moment, considering who to call.

Then he started to dial Dave. Just as he was about to punch in the last digit, he froze, realizing that connecting this call would change everything. He looked back in the direction where Leia had disappeared and knew how much change would happen in her world because of this call. He frowned, looking down at the number, and slowly let his finger off the last digit. Was he ready for that? He was stronger, and he was certainly to the point where he could leave.

What would he say to the rest of the world out there waiting for him, if he didn't go back now? Questions would be asked, like why had he held off letting them know where he was and that he was alive, recuperating, and would return as soon as he could. Knowing he couldn't delay this, he quickly redialed, and, when a voice came on the other end, he spoke. "Dave?"

"Yes, who is this?"

"It's Bullard."

After a moment of shocked silence on the other end of the phone, then a roar ripped through it. "Bullard? Dear God, where are you?" he said, breathless. "I'm coming to get you right now."

"I'm not exactly sure where I am, but I am alive and getting better," he said. "Recovery has been rough. My memory is finally coming back. I just got my hands on a cell phone now too," he added. "I'm on one of the smaller islands somewhere in the South Pacific."

"I'm out here too," Dave said, excitement and relief in his voice. "My God, after all this time …" He paused. "I've been going from place to place, looking for any man who had been picked up out of the water," he said. "I had one more I was checking on, and I just hadn't gotten there yet. We were trying to lock down a better location for him."

"Well, it's probably me," he said, with a note of humor.

"I'm coming," he said. "Can anybody there give me any directions?" As Bullard turned around, he saw Leia standing there, her bottom lip trembling. Immediately he closed his eyes and said, "I'll get back to you on that. Just know that I'm getting better and that I'm alive. Hey, I still don't know what happened, do you?"

"There's a hell of a lot to fill you in on," Dave said, his tone deep and dark. "Don't presume that you're safe even now. Most of the team has been hit as they've been chasing leads, trying to figure out what the hell is going on and what happened to you."

"Well, nobody made it here."

"No, the team has focused their energies on trying to figure out who was trying to take you out in the first place," he said. "I'm the one who's been tracking you down."

"Ryland and Garret?"

"They're both alive," Dave rushed to assure him. "They were also badly hurt in the plane crash, but they're alive."

"Thank God for that," Bullard said, pinching the bridge of his nose. "You can't understand how good it is to hear your voice and to know those boys are okay. The team means a lot to me."

"And you to them," Dave said. "You're sure nobody there can give me information to help me find you?"

Leia must have overheard because she stepped forward and held out her hand. He took a deep breath and spoke to her. "It's Dave, my best man."

His wording was strange to her, but she accepted it and spoke into the phone. "My name is Leia," she said, "and we're on one of the islands outside of Thailand."

"Where exactly are you?" he asked.

She gave him directions that gave Bullard a much better

idea of where he was.

"Did you find and rescue him?" Dave asked.

She handed the phone back to Bullard, then turned and walked away, not answering Dave's question.

"It's me again, Dave," Bullard said.

"I'll be there tomorrow," he said.

"Make it the day after," Bullard said. "I have a little bit of healing to do here yet."

"I still can't believe it," Dave said. "Jesus."

"I feel the same way, man. It feels like I'm connected to the world again."

"You are. I promise I'll be there as soon as I can." With that, he hung up.

Bullard stood here for a long moment, the phone against his chest, realizing how momentous this one phone call was. Not only would he get his life back and be reunited with the people in the world he cared about, but he would also lose somebody he cared about here. Somebody he hadn't expected to care for. He hadn't realized how difficult this would be, until now that they were at this point in time.

He looked over to find that Leia had disappeared. He winced at that. He couldn't stay here forever though. And, as much as she said it was her world, he wasn't sure that it was as much her world as it was the place she hid in. He was sorry for that too, because obviously a ton of pain and trauma of some kind held her back. He would like to do whatever he could to get her back into the real world, but, more than that, he wanted to take her with him and to show her that the rest of the world wasn't all filled with assholes. In order to do that, he might have to dig a little deeper into who she was and what had gone on in her life.

He called Dave back. "I don't know anything about

her," he said, "but can you look into it quietly for me?"

"I will," he promised. "She's a heart surgeon?"

"Yes, and I got the impression that she's from the US. I don't know anything else about it. And I can't confirm her last name. So that ads to the problem. But I'm sending a picture."

"Got it," Dave said. "Ice's father might know something."

"Right." And Bullard realized that was who he should have called in the first place. But his feelings were a little mixed up in that quarter, and he wasn't sure why. After hanging up with Dave, Bullard turned and headed toward Leia's place. "I'll go for a swim," he called into the cabin.

"Okay," she said, "just don't overdo it."

She was always watching out for him; that was one thing about her, how she never quite let up. "Will do," he said, knowing that any other answer would just make her worry, and he didn't want to do that. He headed to the river and slipped into the water, using the stronger current as a means to power up. He swam against it until he got too tired, and then he let it push him down toward the opening of the river. Around the corner, he hauled himself up onto the rocks and walked back across.

It was such a gorgeous location and such a beautiful place to be that he saw why she didn't want to leave. It was sheltered and had been a home for her when she needed one. Obviously she hadn't had anybody else here to help her and nobody who could get her where she needed to be at that time. He felt sorry for her for that, having to heal all on her own, and again letting him help her now was not something that she would accept from him. She was stubborn and prideful—something else he understood full well—but he wanted answers, and he wanted to find a solution to bring her home with him.

At that, Ice's face flashed before him. Dear beloved Ice, a woman like none other. A woman he cared about, who was so incredibly strong. If Levi wasn't there for her, Bullard would have snatched her up in a heartbeat. But Levi was there, and something tugged in the corner of his memory. They were starting a family, which was another reason Bullard needed to walk away and to find a life without her. Because he couldn't spend his whole lifetime sitting in Ice's background because Bullard knew Ice would never walk away from Levi willingly.

And for the first time Bullard realized how much of his life he'd been silently waiting for Ice. Not that he wished Levi ill; they were close friends, but Bullard knew he could never have more with Ice. But this time with Leia had shown him that it was time for something new and different. As he turned to stare back up at the cabin where Leia was, he knew exactly what he wanted, but he would have a hard time convincing her that he was what she wanted and needed too.

CHAPTER 6

THE NEXT MORNING Leia rose, dry-eyed, having not slept much during the night. She had gotten up several times to look into the bushes, realizing that his world had already infiltrated hers. She had gotten him a phone, and he had immediately contacted the outside world, and now everything was coming undone. She went for a swim, letting herself float down to the mouth of the river, before sitting on one of her favorite rocks, staring out at the world around her. Somehow it had all gone to hell, and she needed to just get through these next few days.

Because she knew he'd be gone at that point. He would leave so damn fast that it would make her head spin. But then why wouldn't he? He had people out there, waiting and hoping that he had survived, and he had. She probably should have contacted people earlier, but she'd been selfish, keeping him to herself. She gave a broken laugh at that. What a fool. She had no excuse. She could have sent word to the world, but she thought it was wrong to do so and had followed that instinct, but even now it sounded foolish to her ears, like she was some dried-up old maid, pinning her hopes on this one person.

And here he was leaving. Of course he was leaving; he had no reason to stay. This wasn't his world. Giving herself a headshake and bolstering her confidence, she turned and headed back to the cabin. She had a quick cold shower and then shucked her bathing suit for a long flowing dress. She didn't know if people would arrive today or not, but she figured that anybody trying to find him would be here as soon as possible. She set out breakfast as she always did, and, when there was no sign of him, she walked down to check on him, but he was gone. She frowned, calling out, "Bullard? Are you here?"

But still no answer. She wondered if he'd already left, without saying goodbye. Her heart constricted at the thought—until she heard him call out behind her, and she spun to see him coming up from the water. Somehow they just missed each other. "Breakfast is ready," she said.

He nodded, his gaze searching. "Did you get any sleep?"

"Not much," she said quietly. "Did you?"

"No," he growled. "I don't want to leave."

That stopped her in her tracks. She turned to look at him. "Then don't."

"That won't happen," he said. "I have a life out there, several companies, property."

"Good for you." She turned to get water from her place. "I'll put on the coffee." She half expected him to grab her and haul her around to talk to him because he had that kind of look on his face. But he didn't. He let her go. She wasn't sure if she was sad about that or not. Obviously they were at some impasse, and neither knew how to move forward. She was just as guilty—being like a robot, as she had for months, years even, feeling the pain inside that she couldn't even begin to explore. She dared not verbalize it because she felt she would shatter as soon as it came to light. She set out coffee and breakfast.

When he stepped up on her porch, he nodded and sat

down beside her. "You could come with me."

"I don't belong in your world," she murmured. But her heart wondered if she could fit in. She didn't really know him that well, and, given the circumstances with a man of his obvious means, she wasn't sure she wanted to.

"You could if you wanted to," he said, reiterating her own thoughts.

"Maybe," she said, "but you have a life back there. I don't. I haven't got the means to make a living, and I'm not even sure I'm ready to go back to society."

"To the society that hurt you?"

"To the society I chose not to live in," she said quietly. "Judge me all you want, but that world I don't particularly want to have anything to do with anymore."

"I get it," he said. "Honestly I do. But, Leia, you can't just hide away here forever."

"I have been doing it for a long time, so why can't I?" she asked him curiously.

"Because you became a surgeon for a reason. To help people."

"But not everybody wants to be helped," she said, tilting her face to the sun and closing her eyes, searching for that sense of equilibrium she tried so hard to achieve and was so terrified to let go of now that she had found it.

"I care about you," he said abruptly.

She opened her eyes, smiled at him. "I know," she said, "and I care about you. But that doesn't mean we move forward."

"That's as damn good a reason as any," he said, growling at her.

She nodded. "You'll have to go back to your world and see what matters."

"Exactly. And you need to try my world to see if it's something you can live with. You can't make a decision from here, any more than I can make a decision if I don't go back there."

There was a certain craftiness to his voice, and she realized he'd been thinking about this as an argument for a long time. Smiling, she said, "We'll see."

And, with that, he had to be content because she wasn't willing to give him anymore. At least not yet. When a commotion came outside as they were finishing breakfast, he looked at her, and she sighed.

"It sounds like your company has arrived."

His face lit up, and he bolted to his feet and raced around the corner. She watched from a few steps back as a stranger, looking like he'd been given a new lease on life, came around the corner. With open arms, the two men fell into each other's arms. She was amazed to see such joy and love on their faces.

Who was this man who brought Bullard such joy? She hadn't known that he cared so much about someone, likely several someones, she realized, remembering his face when he talked about his team. But apparently he had a huge love of life and a love for others in that big frame of his.

As soon as Bullard pulled back, he turned and motioned at Leia. "This is Leia," he said. "She rescued me and kept me alive all this time. She brought me back from the brink of death. Leia, this is Dave. We served in the same unit in the military, and we've been working together ever since."

Dave immediately stepped closer and gave her the gentlest of hugs. "You have my undying thanks," he said, "and, if we can do anything for you, please let us know. Bullard is a very special person, and our world was a much dimmer place when we began to lose hope of finding him after all this time."

"I probably should have contacted the outside world earlier," she admitted. "But it seemed much easier to stay safe in this cocoon, than to face whatever forces sent his plane into the ocean." Dave nodded, his gaze searching and gentle, and she felt as if he saw so much more than she wanted him to. But she smiled at him bravely instead. "He has asked me to return with him, just so you know."

"In that case, I would be extremely honored to have you come back with us," he said, his gaze going from one to the other.

"I haven't said I will," she said. "This is my world here."

"I understand that, but your old world could be yours again, if you wanted it to be."

She stiffened and glared at Bullard. "Yours is the world of danger and ugliness."

"But yours was just as ugly in another way," he said, "and nobody was there to help you. I won't let that happen again."

Shaking her head, she said, "You don't know anything about it."

"No, I don't," he said, "but I trust Dave to find out."

She nodded stiffly and said, "In that case, you guys can go talk but don't involve me." With that, she spun on her heel and walked away.

"SHE'S A VERY interesting woman," Dave said in admiration. "But trust you to find somebody out in the middle of nowhere."

"I didn't know anything but her for the longest time,"

Bullard said. "I had no memories, and she wouldn't give me even a hint. She was very cautious about me trying to force them to return."

"As you well know," Dave said, "you're much better off to just let them fall back into place on their own."

"Yes, but it was frustrating," he said.

Dave looked at him. "Do you think she was keeping you here deliberately?"

"No," he said. "Things only just started to fall into place over the last couple weeks, after I turned a corner physically, able to move a bit on my own," he said. "Leia did surgery on me right here."

At that, Dave grinned. "I hope you didn't lose anything of importance."

Bullard howled with laughter. "Nope," he said, "but I haven't tested everything."

"You haven't given it a test drive, huh?"

"I've been trying to move gently," he said, turning to look where she'd gone. "She's a very special woman, and she's been badly hurt."

"Yeah, I can give you some details on part of her past. She's Leia Montrose. Thirty-four years old. Her birthday is April 2nd. She was a surgeon, was up for a chief surgery position. Because of her age, there was significant opposition, but she was one of those super-talented surgeons."

"What happened?" Bullard asked, anxious to find out.

"She was assisting the surgery of a high-profile patient. Long story short, the patient didn't make it, and she was blamed. Her version was that the lead surgeon deliberately killed the patient on the table, while she tried hard to save him."

"Ouch," he said. "And nobody else saw what he did?"

"No, and he said she did it, while she said it was him. He was a senior surgeon, highly respected in his field, but vocal in his opposition to her advancement."

"And all that was enough for her to just walk away?"

"It was highly publicized, and the public reviled her," Dave said. "She was blamed for the death of a high-profile patient. The hospital canceled her surgical position, and somehow it was leaked to the media that there was talk of a murder charge. She was crucified," he said simply. "The hospital turned on their own rising star to deflect attention away from them."

"Good Lord. No wonder she doesn't want to go back. She'd have to face it all over again."

"Yes. Unless something could be done to prove her innocence and to expose that conspiracy against her," Dave said, giving Bullard an encouraging look.

"I don't think she's up for the fight," Bullard said. "She hasn't got the heart for it."

"No. Sometimes life is like that," Dave said. "But maybe we should pick up her fight?"

"I would love to, but I don't want to alienate her either, getting her involved regardless, and you know she would have to be a party to the legal fight."

"We've seen injustice all over the world."

"Yeah, we sure have." Bullard looked around and said, "Please tell me the rest of the team is okay. How bad has it been?"

"No deaths," Dave said, "though we've had close calls and some serious injuries. Everybody is recovering, some slowly, but we're still on the hunt. If you've got a couple hours, I can bring you up to date on what's gone on."

"I've got nothing but time," he said. "Did you arrange

for us to get out of here?"

"Yeah. I have a boat and a helicopter on standby," he said. "I wasn't sure what I was up against coming here."

"I'm not sure either," Bullard said. "We've also had some strangers lurking around the island. More than usual apparently," he said. "People have been hiding in the bushes watching, and you know how I feel about that."

"You also have a beautiful woman here," Dave said. "I'm sure she's attracted plenty of looks."

"Maybe, but it feels like it's more than that."

"Good enough," Dave said. "I'll still trust your instincts. Injured or not, you've always had an uncanny ability in that department."

"Dave, do we know who blew up the plane?"

"Well, we know one layer," he said. Then they sat down together and, for several hours, went through everything Dave knew, as methodically as he could. By the time he gratefully accepted the fresh juice from Leia who'd come to join them, his voice was raspy and dry.

She stared at him in shock, after hearing only part of it, but understood how immense the trials against Bullard's team had been. "It's a miracle any of the team is alive," she murmured.

"It's a miracle he's alive," Dave said, pointing to Bullard, "and believe me. We're all very grateful for what you've done."

She just shrugged and walked away to give them some room, still within hearing distance but not close enough to intrude.

"So we're still looking for the very top man. Is that it?" Bullard asked.

"Yes," Dave said. "We've finally got it down to that, after going through layers and layers of crap to get here."

"I can't believe Deedee is dead."

"I know," Dave said, "and to think Kano and Catherine are together because of it."

"Well, I wouldn't say they're together because of it. They were together before, and Deedee essentially broke them up," Bullard said. "She was one hell of a bitch." But there was almost a note of respect and admiration in his voice as he said it.

"We were worried for a while there that you had something going with her," Dave said.

"No," he said, shaking his head and looking at Leia, who was close enough to hear. "There were just some things you couldn't do with her. Lines not to be crossed. She was a black widow if there ever was one."

"Apparently she did kill a couple husbands. Michael has survived and is still holding the reins of Kingdom Securities, though several of their men went rogue and have gone off the reservation. But the thing about this deal is, at every step of the way, every low-level bad guy has been taken out by the upper-level bad guys. Total clean-up from within. So we still don't know who's at the top, but we're finally at the last level. Although everyone said it's someone close enough to all of us that we'd stay with him in your absence."

"There aren't too many who could be at the top," Bullard said. "And since it isn't Deedee, and it's not Michael, I'm not sure who else among my competitors it could be," he admitted.

"That's the thing," Dave said. "We've all been wondering who this unnamed person could be."

Bullard nodded. "Have you called the rest of the team?"

"Absolutely. Several are on their way because they don't

believe it, so you can expect more company," he said.

"Well, they need to bring supplies," he said. "We don't have a ton here, definitely not as much as those guys eat."

Dave nodded and pulled out his phone. "I'll give them word on that," he said. "Izzie really wants to see you as well."

"Ah, Izzie. We have some time to make up for. Nothing like sitting here and thinking about the things that you could have done differently," he said. "I didn't do well by her."

At that, Leia smiled and joined them.

"Dave found out some of your history. Sounds like you were made a scapegoat. What would you have done differently?" Bullard asked her pointedly.

"I'm not sure I could have done anything differently," she said. "When somebody is out to set you up, how do you get away from it?"

He nodded. "So, I presume you didn't kill the patient?"

"No, I didn't kill him," she said. "It wasn't my knife close to an artery, but Leo had his right there."

"And you think he did it?"

"He looked right at me before he sliced it," she said, "and it wasn't a random slice, like an accidental nick. It was a long gash in a major artery. We couldn't save him at that point."

"I'm sorry," he said. "And you, being the young upstart, were reviled and blamed, right?"

"Particularly when Leo said I had done it, and he'd watched me do it. Nobody would listen to me over him," she said. "It was all his word against mine, and, although I was a respected surgeon there and thought I had a strong support system, when push came to shove, nobody was there for me. I could have moved somewhere else or done something else, but I didn't want to. I wanted to just walk away and not get involved in anything where my hand could be blamed for killing someone again."

"Do you have any tiny shred of doubt that you were involved at all?"

"Meaning, did I wonder if somehow I had sliced his artery? No, I have no doubt about how things went down, and I was not involved," she said. "I protested until I was blue in the face, but nobody believed me. When they started talking murder charges, I was asked to leave, and I left. They said they would do their best to mitigate any malpractice suits against me, as long as I disappeared. So I did. I up and left, then came here, and here is where I've been ever since."

"You were one of the best and the brightest surgeons of your time, according to the media," Dave said.

"Yes," she said, "back then maybe I was, but things change, and I'm out of practice now."

"Except for me, you practiced on me," Bullard said.

She nodded, her gaze shrouded. "Yes, though it's not like I had much choice. You were dying. Even then, under these primitive conditions, there was no guarantee that I wouldn't kill you in the process."

"And did you operate on anybody local?" Dave asked.

She shrugged. "Only for minor issues. Never anything major."

"But you could if need be?"

"I could," she said, "but I won't."

"Unless it's an emergency," Bullard said.

She glared at him. "I'm not going back to practicing like I did before," she snapped. "Nothing you can say will make me do that."

"No, I wouldn't pressure you either," he said. "There's nothing like broken trust."

"It doesn't heal," she said. "You're always left to wonder and worry."

"What if we could do something to exonerate you?"

"Nobody will care," she said, staring off in the distance. "Nobody even remembers my name by now."

"Maybe," Bullard said, "but somebody got away with murder."

"It wasn't the first time," she said quietly. "It definitely wasn't the first time."

CHAPTER 7

L EIA WASN'T AT all sure she could go back and face an inquiry like that again. She had been absolutely gutted to have had so many of her cohorts throw her under the bus. As the one friend had said, "A bright young light rising rapidly within their ranks wasn't something the old establishment could handle, so they'd done what they could to squash her effectively."

But Leia had never suspected that anyone would have actually murdered a patient on the table in order to get her out of there. She didn't want anything to do with a world like that. Bullard spoke about exoneration, but all she saw was an extension of the pain, and it wouldn't help anyone. Should her associate have been brought to justice? Absolutely. Would it come to that? Not likely. She didn't have much faith in the system anymore. It was just one of those things about life that wouldn't come together. She looked from Dave to Bullard. "I agree that he should probably be charged," she said quietly, "but it's not like there is any validity in whatever I say."

"They don't tape any of those surgeries?"

"Yes," she said, "but somehow"—and her tone turned very dry—"the tape went missing."

Dave's eyes widened. "That is completely unconscionable," he said.

"That is the industry," she said quietly, "and, no, I didn't know it before I headed into the field. I went in with the naive impression that I could help people."

"You still can," Bullard said quietly. "I need a good surgeon." At that, Dave looked at him in surprise.

She looked at Dave and asked, "What's his skill level in that field?"

Dave shrugged. "He's very talented. We have a full OR at home, with some of the most incredible equipment you would ever hope to work with."

Leia found herself intrigued in spite of herself. "My skills are too rusty," she said immediately, backing off again.

"The only thing that's rusty," Bullard said, "is your confidence, and not in yourself or your skills but in the people around you."

"With good reason."

"Absolutely, and I'm not trying to make you feel threatened," he said. "But you do need to return and face whatever you've been running from, one way or another."

"No, I don't," she said. "I have a wonderfully peaceful life here. Why would I want to change that?"

"Maybe because it's not what you were intended to do," he said. "Like you said, you got into medicine to help people." He looked at Dave. "How are things with the clinic?"

"Ugly," he said, "we closed the doors almost immediately because we didn't have anybody to work there."

"What about your niece?"

"We're trying to convince her to come back when she finishes her current commitment," he said. "Oh, and she's hooked up with Fallon now, by the way."

Bullard stared at him in surprise. "Wow," he said, with a

chuckle. "You know what? I can almost see that. They were always wary around each other, weren't they?"

"Absolutely they were," Dave said, with a smirk. "Honestly I am thrilled because I want to keep her close."

"Of course," Bullard said, with a nod. "We've all had such grave losses that sometimes you don't see how to come back from it."

Leia looked at Dave, curious. "I don't know anything about you or your life," she said.

Dave shrugged. "Let's just say I lost my family, and it took me a long time to recover."

"I'm so sorry. I can't imagine," she said, with feeling, "but having no one left to support you must have been doubly difficult."

Dave nodded, looking at her. "Did you have no family to help you out?"

"My father was a gifted surgeon, and he had a heart attack on the job. People said that he was the reason I was hired, his recommendation, I mean. But he passed away soon afterward."

"Ah, and people don't like that, do they?"

"No, they don't," she said. "I was also trying to do some fairly difficult surgeries with him, and people didn't like that either."

"So what about your mother?"

"She left my father and ended up with a second marriage and a second family, this time with children who weren't quite so ambitious, just like she wanted. She wanted children who would turn around and have more children, so she could become a grandmother. She wasn't interested in having a career woman in her world."

"How did that work out for her?"

"It's a little early to tell," she said, "but she has four sons now, so, in that sense, she got exactly what she wanted. No more career-seeking daughters."

"Kind of sad in a way," Dave said. "Having ambition is not a negative. It's all about what you do in life and the gift of what you leave behind. We're only here for a short time, so to sit here and do nothing but procreate—not even using their gifts—seems like a waste. I guess it works for some people, but the world needs all of us and our gifts that we can offer."

"But not everybody wants you to use your gifts," she said quietly, "as I found out, far too late."

"You were a double threat to the establishment," he said. "If your father had lived, he might have been able to save you. He probably didn't realize the extent of the competition against you."

"No, I don't think so. He didn't really see humans and their failings. He only saw aortas and ventricles and cranial cavities," she said. "He was very much into his work. The fact that I was too gave us a bond, but otherwise—without that—we probably wouldn't have been close."

"Was he upset over the divorce?"

"I think it was more of a minor inconvenience to him, but thankfully she handled everything, so he didn't have to leave the office."

Even Bullard winced at that. "That must have made it even more difficult for you."

"Well, it certainly gave me a disassociated feeling about the whole thing. The fact that she remarried within weeks of the divorce being finalized said a lot about where she was at."

"So she was already moving on," Dave said. "We've seen that happen time and time again."

"Exactly, and it left me in a weird place," she said. "I wasn't finished with my education, but I was doing as much as I could in practicums soon afterward. I did volunteer work constantly, overseas and at home, spending every waking hour in an operating room, or outside the OR, prepping people to go in."

"Your life must have been very difficult when she walked away."

"It was chaotic at first," she said, "but also relief in a sense because I knew I was such a disappointment to her."

"You shouldn't have let your self-confidence be shaken that way," Dave scolded.

"It wasn't a lack of faith in my skills. It was like Bullard said," she stated, with half a smile, "it was my confidence in the people around me that was shaken. In many ways I had been like my father, very narrow-minded, controlled, and centered on only what I was doing with my hands. I wasn't so worried about the people around me, about maintaining relationships with coworkers and things like that. Maybe I was as difficult as my father was. I don't know. My hospital demise came so quickly, I didn't really get a chance to sort it all out."

"I'm sorry," Dave said.

"It doesn't matter," she said, staring off in the distance. "It's easy to look back in hindsight and realize that I was probably not terribly nice to be around. I don't know." She shrugged. "I didn't see what was coming at me, so I was blindsided by it all. That made it very difficult."

"Of course. Do you mind if I make a few more inquiries?"

She looked at Dave in surprise. "About what?" she asked. "I'm a nobody. Nonexistent. I don't even live in the world anymore."

"Great, then you won't have a problem with me making those inquiries," he said.

Just the thought made her stomach heave a little bit, but she studied him for a long moment, then acquiesced. "I guess it won't hurt. But don't expect to find anything."

"No," he said, "not at all."

She looked at him, frowned, and said, "You said that a little too fast."

At that, he gently said, "Don't worry about it."

She shook her head. "That's not likely to happen either," she said, smiling.

"You never know," he said. "Life can be difficult for many people. But that doesn't mean that it'll be the end. What it can show you is a whole new way to live."

"And I found that right here," she said gently. "Remember?"

"You're existing," he said, shaking his head, "but you're not thriving."

"You're not a shrink," she said, "and I've spent a lot of time in introspection, finally getting to the point where I could live quite happily like this, and I don't need anybody to tell me that I can't."

"Of course not," Dave said, "that would be like waving a red flag at a bull. In many ways you're like Bullard here."

She frowned at that, but Bullard was grinning broadly. "You seem to think that's a compliment," she said, puzzled.

"Having a group around me has given me ample opportunity to see my good side and my bad side," he said. "And they aren't always that easy to contemplate. I want you to come back with me," he said.

She shrugged. The one thing she didn't want was to have

him do something like that out of guilt. She wanted so much more and didn't know how to say it. She wasn't even sure they had anything real here to build on. "I don't think that's a good idea," she finally said.

"So you've said before," he said. "I suggest we ignore the *should*s or the *said*s or the *would*s and just go ahead and do it."

"That's because you're like a bull in a china shop," she said, "and you have this thing about getting what you want, without considering anyone else."

He looked at her and started to laugh. "I haven't even been conscious all that long," he said, "at least not with my brain intact, and look at how well you know me."

"You're just cheeky," she murmured. Then she turned and headed to her cabin. "You guys have a lot to talk about. I'll give you some privacy to do that."

"Pack," he instructed.

"Nope, not likely," she said, without even turning around. Then she disappeared into her cabin. As soon as she was alone, she sat down on the corner of her bed and pressed her hands against her eyes, willing the tears to stay back. It was one thing to live here with him. It was another thing entirely to leave this idyllic hideaway for something un-known and potentially very painful. As she sat here quietly, she heard an odd noise. Turning around, she saw a stranger at her door.

She stood, looked at him, and asked, "What can I do for you? Who are you?"

He didn't look like any islander she knew, and he wasn't dressed like it. He was dressed like a foreigner. Like Dave. But the look on his face was nowhere near as happy or as kind. He smiled an overly familiar smile that made her almost freeze inside, and she wondered if she knew him, but she couldn't place his face. It was like a fractured version of some other face. Then she noted the scars all over his features.

"Are you okay?" she asked, stepping closer.

He looked at her in surprise, then lifted a hand to his face. "Yes, I'm fine," he said, "but thank you for noticing."

She shook her head. "Why are you here?"

"I came to see you," he said, but nothing terribly awe-inspiring was about that voice.

"Why?"

"You have something of mine," he said quietly. She looked at him in surprise and then looked around. "I don't have anything at all."

"No, you just didn't know that what you had was so important," he said, "but now that I've found it, I do feel compelled to make a few changes."

Feeling like he was talking in some weird crypto-language, she stared at him for a moment, feeling her instincts kick in. She was a bit slow after the emotional set-to with Bullard yet soon realized that not only was this guy here for her but he wasn't here for any good reason at all.

"I think you need to leave," she said harshly. "I don't know who or what you think you're after, but you're not welcome here."

"Ah," he said, "you're finally clued in, aren't you?"

She shook her head. "No, I don't have a clue what you're doing," she said, "or why you're even here, but there's nothing about you that makes me feel safe."

"Good," he said, "because I'm definitely not here to make your day."

Shocked, she didn't know what to say.

"Instead," he said, "I'm here to make sure somebody else's day takes a turn." And, with that, he lunged forward, slapped a hand over her mouth and pinched her neck. And slowly, almost like in the comics, she sagged in his arms, until she was on the floor. He picked her up while she was barely conscious and threw her over his shoulder, then disappeared into the trees.

BULLARD AND DAVE finally fell silent, after both had been talking so fast, trying to fill each other in on what had happened. Dave had been doing the bulk of the talking, but then he had asked about Leia, and that had started another whole conversation.

Bullard took several long slow deep breaths. "It's been really good to be here," he said. "It's been a step out of the craziness of my normal world that I hadn't realized I needed."

"I kept telling you that you needed to take more time off," Dave said.

"I hear you," Bullard replied.

"But you haven't been really hearing me. You've just been listening on a surface level."

Bullard groaned and rolled his eyes. "Okay, so the world forced me to slow down."

"Exactly. And now it's a matter of slowly getting back in, and realizing how much and what you want to do, plus how much you don't want to do."

"I want to ease back and not do as much traveling, and I don't want to be as heavily involved."

"Let's face it," Dave said. "A lot of what you were doing was filling your time and your mind, while trying to forget

Ice and all that."

"I don't want to forget Ice," Bullard said quietly. "She's a very special part of me, and she always will be."

"Yes, but you didn't allow yourself room to find anybody else," he said.

"Maybe so." He shrugged. "But it feels like that was a long time ago."

"And I think that's why this break was so important for you. Honestly I'm surprised at how well you've matched up with Leia. The fact that she saved your life is also a pretty positive thing and of course builds a bond that you may not have expected," Dave said. "But, at the same time, it's also given you a chance to get to know her. Before, you had short relationships, more of a stress relief than anything. Women were all over you, more than willing to become something more, but you couldn't see them."

"Not sure I do now either," he said.

"No," Dave said, with a smile, "but that's because you also see Leia now."

He looked at Dave and asked, "What do you think about her coming back with me?"

"I think that would be lovely. We do need to look into her history though, and I've already started the team on it," he said.

"Good. I think it's completely wrong for somebody to accuse her of something like that, only to find out that they actually committed murder in order to get rid of her."

"The other thing you have to consider," Dave said, "is the fact that it's all too possible," and he hesitated.

"*All too possible*, what?"

Dave took a deep breath. "You don't really know Leia."

Bullard glared at him, though he knew better than to

immediately jump in and defend her because Dave was right; Bullard didn't know Leia. Yet he did. He knew her in the way anybody who'd survived a traumatizing event knew the person who cared for them selflessly the way that she had, day in and day out. But he also knew that Dave wouldn't have seen it, wouldn't have known it. And he still would be the pragmatist that said Bullard really didn't know who she was. He stared out at the ocean, and his jaw twitched.

"I know it's not something you want to hear," Dave said, "and it's not something that I want to bring up either. But the facts remain. You do not know her that well, and, for all you know, she's lying."

"Check with Ice," he said suddenly. "Her father's in the industry, so he would probably know something about it."

"That's a good idea," Dave said, pulling out his phone. He immediately sent off texts.

"Did you tell Ice?"

"Hell yes, I told her," he said. "She's been screaming for joy ever since she found out. Terk has been looking for you. Even telling her that you were alive. Plus, he's the one who said he had found you."

Something settled inside Bullard. "I'm glad to hear that. Terk is something else," he said softly. "Ice will always be special."

"She will," Dave said. "But it's also time for you to find something more for yourself."

He looked at him, looked up in the direction of Leia's cabin, and said, "Yes, I think you're right. And I think Leia is it."

"Good," Dave said. "You would make me very happy if that was the case."

Bullard looked at his old friend and smirked. "Even if I

don't know her?"

"By the time we're done analyzing her background and tearing her life apart," he said, "it won't make much difference." Immediately Bullard frowned at him. Dave chuckled. "You know what I mean."

"I know," he said, "but I wouldn't want to hurt her."

"We're not in the business of pulling wings off butterflies," Dave said, "but, if we've got black widows flying around, you can bet that we'll take care of them appropriately."

Bullard rolled his eyes at that. "She's not a black widow."

"We'll find out soon enough," he said. At that, Bullard stood slowly and stretched. Dave assessed him carefully.

"I'm better," Bullard said. "Not in peak form yet by any means, and I've just slowly started rebuilding the muscles, but you and I both know I'm not there."

"But you'll get there," he said.

"Maybe. I'm not sure if I'll ever get back to where I was though."

"Do you know how badly you were hurt?"

"No," he said. "I have no memory except that chaotic moment of the plane exploding."

"And you just woke up here?"

"I woke up here, completely incapacitated and tied down in many ways," he said. "I don't know all the details, but I had a very broken body," he said. "I was very blessed that she was the one who found me."

"Interesting that she didn't let anybody know."

"I think that even then she knew," Bullard said.

"Knew what?" Dave asked, confused.

"That I had been targeted," he said quietly. "She was always about secrecy."

"That's kind of creepy, isn't it?"

"Maybe, but I'll take it because she kept me alive." He frowned, looked at his buddy, and said, "Speaking of which, she should have come back by now."

"Missing her so soon?" he teased.

"I haven't gone more than one conscious hour without seeing her all this time," he said.

"But she's also got to deal with some difficult problems herself right now. She's got a lot to think about."

"And I didn't want it to be difficult for her, Dave. I really didn't."

"You can't save everybody," he said.

"I know. But I'd like to save those who helped me."

"Well, speaking of that, an awful lot of guys are on their way here."

"They don't need to do that," he said, turning to look at him. "I'll be heading home."

"That's an awful lot of traveling, and honestly I'm not sure you're up for it yet."

Bullard glared at him. "Where's the jet?"

"You mean, your friend's private jet?"

He stopped, thought about it, and said, "Oh, yeah, that's right. I saw trips in a private jet and assumed it was mine. But now the puzzle pieces are falling into place on that. I don't own it, do I?"

"Nope. But you have some very grateful people around you, people you have helped. They made certain you have equipment available to you whenever you need it."

"Right," Bullard said. "I saved his daughter, didn't I?"

"Yes, you did," Dave said, with a smile. "And his second wife."

"Interesting," he said. "Funny how we block things out."

"You blocked a lot of that one out regardless," he said. "Some of it was too painful."

"Did I get hurt?"

"No," he said, "but we had one of the only two deaths we've ever had in the business."

Bullard winced at that. "Pierre. It's all coming back now, and that was a long time ago."

"Yeah, it was. So, back to the jet, he only uses it once or twice a year, but he keeps it because it's kind of like his first car. He doesn't want to let it go, so you get to use it whenever because he rarely uses it himself."

"Sounds like a good deal to me." Looking puzzled for a moment, Bullard scratched his head, then looked up to the cabin again. "Something's off."

"Oh, your instincts are back up to snuff, are they?"

"Not by a long shot," he said, "but something isn't right." Immediately he walked toward Leia's cabin.

"If you're not quite up to par, maybe you shouldn't be barging in there," Dave murmured.

"Maybe not, but I also don't feel very good not checking things out."

"Well, we could always ..." Dave trailed off because Bullard wasn't listening anymore.

"Something's wrong, Dave." He bounced up the few steps to the porch outside her place and stepped in. It was completely empty.

"Where would she go?" Dave asked. "Where would she go on the island?"

"Anywhere," he said, "but she wouldn't have left for long without checking in with me." Dave looked at him, and he shook his head. "Don't give me that look. I know this woman. You don't."

"No, I don't," Dave said. "What is it you think has happened?"

Bullard turned to look around, then frowned. Then he pointed out footprints. "Look, a man's boot print." He looked over Dave.

"Not mine," Dave said, "because I haven't been up there." He walked over to the other footsteps and pointed out, "Looks like a bit of a scuffle here, Bullard. And deeper footprints afterward."

"She's been forcefully taken," he said in shock.

"Looks like it," Dave said, as he turned and headed down, following the tracks. Bullard joined him, and the two of them tracked the footprints to a small bay on the side.

"I didn't even know this little bay was here," he said. "God, I've been living in this idyllic prison, one so gentle and soft that I let my instincts down. And now some asshole's come in and snatched her."

"But you don't know that it is related to you," Dave said quietly. "And we don't know that's what happened. I'll keep tracking these prints."

"Who else would it be related to?" he said, glaring at Dave.

"There could be all kinds of things in her own history, remember? It's not as simple as it might have once looked."

Bullard stopped at that. "Did you hear back from Ice?"

"No, not yet."

Bullard held out his hand. "Let me see the phone." Dave immediately passed it over then turned to follow the tracks. Ice was one of the automatic numbers at the top. He quickly punched it, and moments later she answered.

"Dave, how is he?"

"Ice," he said, and for the first time, possibly in his

whole life, he felt the tears creeping up his throat as he heard her voice.

There was split second of silence, and then she gasped. "Oh my God. Bullard, is that you?"

"Yeah, it's me. Damn, it's good to hear your voice."

"Oh my God. We've been searching for you for so damn long." And this time, there was no hiding the tears. She was busy choking them back, as she tried to call out, "Levi, it's Bullard."

Immediately another voice joined the call. "Bullard, what can we do?"

"Dammit, Levi, I just want to hate you, but I can't do it. You're far too good of a man."

"Love you too, bro," Levi said, his own voice choking up. "What can we do to help you from here?"

"Earlier Dave sent a message about Leia, the woman who rescued me and kept me alive for the last few months," he said. "Have you gotten any information at all?"

"I've got a call into my dad, but he hasn't answered me yet," Ice said. "Is it urgent? What's going on?"

"It is now. She's gone missing."

"Missing?" He quickly filled them in on the little bit he knew. "She could be just emotionally traumatized because you're looking at leaving," Ice said cautiously.

"Yeah, I get that," he said. "She could be and likely is, but she's not a runner." There was silence on the other end. "What?"

"Well, she did run," Ice said quietly. "When her world broke up, that's exactly what she did."

"I think it was more a case of walking at that point, walking away from everything important to her."

"Wait, my dad's on the other line," she said. "Hang on

and talk to Levi, I'll be right back."

Levi said, "Do you need a ride? Have you got everything in place to get yourself back home?"

"Dave's here with me," he said looking up as Dave returned a hard look on his face. Bullard's heart sank. That's all the confirmation he needed.

"Oh, good," Levi said, "I imagine half the team's headed that way."

"They shouldn't be," Bullard growled. "On the other hand, if something has happened to Leia, I'll need them."

"Exactly," he said. "Keep your head."

"Planning on it," he said, with a smirk. "A little bit of sanity in this world would be nice."

"I hear you," Levi said. "Your guys have had one hell of a time."

"How about you guys?" Bullard asked.

"Hellish as always," he said. "It seems like the world is just one step away from imploding, at least that's how it feels." Just then Ice came back on.

"Turns out it's a case my father knows well. He knew a lot of the people involved at the time. She was sacrificed, plain and simple," she said, outraged. "He says that Leia is an incredibly gifted surgeon, but the powers that be needed somebody to blame to make it all go away, and they blamed her."

"She says this Leo deliberately murdered the patient with a lengthwise cut to the artery, so they lost him right then and there. He already had a touchy heart, and they had done everything. The other surgeon waited until her hand was in position as well, then did it, blaming her immediately. It was a setup."

There was silence on the other end. "Jesus," Levi said. "A

murder right in front of her."

Bullard's heart sank at the thought of what she'd gone through. "We have to do something about it," he said. "What else does your dad know about it?"

"He only knows the basics," she said, "but he does know a couple people on the board. At the time when he was asking for details, they said it was under wraps."

"Well, it needs to be exposed," Bullard snapped. "That woman saved my life, and she was crucified by the very people she worked beside."

"We've seen it time and time again," Ice said quietly.

"Not this time. If there's one thing I can do for Leia, it's clear her name. At the time, they came close to charging her for murder," he said.

"Yes. That's what my dad was saying," she murmured. "I don't know how bad it was at the time, but apparently a lot of those bigwigs are still very resentful of her."

"But why?"

"She pioneered a new type of surgery, and it was incredibly effective. People don't like it when somebody gets ahead and gets better than themselves."

"Doesn't matter what they like," he snapped. "My God." He felt the anger burning inside. He pinched the bridge of his nose. "I'm so tired of people being shitheads."

"All of us are," Ice said calmly. "So what do you want us to do?"

He smiled. "Good old Ice, right down to business."

"It's why we do what we do," she said happily, "the same as you."

"Right," he said. "Let's pull in as much information as we can on the asshole who committed murder. She said it wasn't the first time."

"What do you mean, not the first time?" she asked.

"Leia said it wasn't the first time he had killed somebody on purpose."

"Oh-ho, in that case," she said, "we need to be on that and fast."

"We'll go take a walk around the island to make sure she'd not just gone for a stroll," he said, "but my heart says it's worse than that."

"Maybe so," she said, "but remember. You're leaving, and, if she cares at all, that will matter. Nobody could look after a patient for all that time, after living alone for five years, without feeling the impending impact of a loss."

He winced at that. "Great, now I need to find her."

"Absolutely," she said, "and I'd love to meet her."

"I'm bringing her back with me," he said, "whether she likes it or not."

At that, Levi chuckled. "Now that sounds like the Bullard I know and love."

When they hung up, Bullard turned to look at Dave to find him already searching the area.

"Hopefully it's just a minor issue and we'll—"

"Oh, she's definitely been taken," Bullard said. "I've got my focus on the ocean and a small boat I can see in the distance."

"She couldn't have been gone too long," Dave replied.

"Just long enough," he said. "And we know that a couple minutes is all it takes and that child you adored, that partner you loved, are gone," Bullard said.

"Right, I'd forgotten you were asshole enough to remind me of that," Dave said, his gaze hard.

"Remind you, hell," Bullard said. "It's been on your mind every damn day since, and don't even try to tell me different, brother."

"I'll give you that," he said, his expression softening. "Listen. I didn't come over here alone. I've got people nearby."

"Good." Bullard turned to look around at the small cabin and said, "Let's go." He headed out, moving as fast as he could, taking nothing with him because he'd arrived with nothing, and he slowly made his way down to the bay.

"The boat will be here soon," Dave said. And he pointed to a skiff coming around the point.

"Ours?"

"I hired it from the mainland."

"Good," he said. "Where are our men?"

"They're coming in a helicopter. We'll meet them over there." Dave pointed.

"How long is the trip?"

"From this side about an hour, an hour and a half. We'll book it though. I'm hoping we can get ahead of this guy so we can pull him over."

"If he's got her in that boat, I'll be so pissed."

"You hold on to that temper, man. I'll be more pissed if she's not in it," he said.

At that, Bullard stopped and looked at him. "We're taking a chance on that, aren't we?" He turned and looked around, shaking his head. "But I don't know where else she could be."

"It's possible she might have gone somewhere, but we did see those scuff marks," Dave said. "And further down there are small steps as if she was set down then picked up again as they disappear after that."

"Doesn't mean that she isn't still on the island, yet how do we take that chance?" Bullard asked.

"We can spend another half hour searching and talking to the islanders to be sure, but, if that boat gets back to the mainland, it'll be damn hard to find her then," Dave said.

Bullard closed his eyes and said, "Get some men to check everywhere on the island. We're going after that boat."

CHAPTER 8

LEIA WOKE UP in a boat, as her body bounced heavily from one side to the other. She was wet, and the wind was chilly. She shivered, wrapping her arms around her light dress, only to find that her hands were tied in front of her. She stared at them in shock and then twisted to see the same stranger from before at the helm of the boat. He couldn't hear over the waves bouncing, and neither could he see her, unless he turned to look. She thought idly of just throwing herself overboard, but it would be certain death. With her hands tied, she didn't have any options at the moment.

Was this man after Bullard? But, if that were the case, why had he taken her? So many questions and she didn't have any answers. She took a slow deep breath, trying to calm her heart. Bullard had no idea where she was. Neither did Dave, and he was new to the island, so he wouldn't understand how things work. She closed her eyes and swore when she realized—of anyone she'd ever known—Bullard of all people knew exactly what to do in a case like this.

So maybe she was lucky after all. She couldn't imagine it would take Bullard long to get back up to speed, since he clearly lived for this kind of action. She'd seen it in his movements, in his need to get fit again, and in the pain in his eyes as he recovered his memories.

An awful lot of dark memories were in his world, ones

that he didn't particularly want to share, but she'd heard so much of it in his nightmares when he had cried out night after night, as she'd sat there, soothing his troubled soul, hearing the pain in his heart. So much about Bullard that she didn't know, but an awful lot she did, and she knew he meant it when he'd said he wanted her to come back with him. But she'd also been worried about this woman named Ice.

Finding out Ice was married had filled Leia with joy, but not if Bullard's heart was still committed to her. Leia wanted him free and clear for herself, which was selfish, but then everybody inherently was. As much as they didn't want to believe it or to even think about it, everything they did was ultimately a reaction to whatever they wanted for themselves. And she couldn't really do anything about that. A little voice in the back of her head said, *Yes, you can. You can survive.*

Because one thing that she knew with absolute clarity was that Bullard wouldn't let her die if he could do something about it. She had to stay alive however she could and wait for him. Because he would come; that was a given. She closed her eyes, her body shivering badly against the cold, as it bounced against another heavy wave. The boat had a decent-size motor, but it wasn't very big for crossing the ocean like this.

She had certainly seen people travel to the mainland in something similar, but they had a lot of skill. She wasn't so sure about this guy. He was running, as if he knew that his life was on fire, and, rightly so, since she knew that, as soon as he was caught, his life would be over.

By kidnapping her, he had forfeited any chance at a future for himself, but she found it very hard to stir up any sympathy for him. The asshole had crossed the wrong person when he had taken someone important to Bullard. Whether it was out of gratitude or love she didn't know, but one thing she knew without a doubt was that Bullard didn't share well or easily. And he would be really pissed when he found her gone. She could only hope that he'd already found out and that this nightmare would be over soon.

ONLY TWENTY MINUTES later, Bullard swore, but, according to Dave, they were forty minutes behind. But they were in the boat and racing as hard and as fast as they could, every bounce jarring his spine and his body. He would feel like hamburger at the end of this day but didn't give a shit. All he wanted to do was pound somebody else into hamburger for frightening poor Leia.

She may have wanted to spend the rest of her life in the peace and harmony of her island, but the real world had intruded, and, whether she liked it or not, it was here now. Whether it was because of him or her own history, he didn't yet know. "Why would they have taken her?"

"My guess is to use as leverage against you."

"Then why not just kill me then," he murmured.

"Because I was there," Dave said. "Maybe he thought the odds weren't good enough. Maybe he thought the rest of the team was there or at least arriving soon."

Bullard frowned at that and then shrugged. "That would make sense maybe. But, if he was that stealthy, he could have just come in, killed me, and left."

"Except I was already here," he reminded him.

"Right." He stared at his old friend. "We need to find her. She must be terrified."

"We will. This guy may have gotten the drop on us and

got out of the gate first," he said, "but remember. We're not alone. We do have people to help us."

Bullard nodded slowly. "And I get that, but it's not enough."

Dave laughed at that. "It's never enough," he said. "That's just a fact of life."

Whoever it was who Dave had hired to get him over here was still piloting the boat, driving it as far forward as he possibly could. Bullard appreciated the speed and the intensity in his gaze as he fought the wind and the ocean. But he didn't trust him. Not one bit. At the moment, he didn't trust anybody. It was a sad return to the real world. Leia had been hiding herself away from the world, but so had he in a way. But now Bullard was back with a vengeance.

Dave stepped up beside him. "Are you okay?"

"I will be," he said, "as soon as I know that she's safe."

"She will be," he said, with a confidence that Bullard couldn't just blindly accept.

"Says you, but we don't even know what's going on," he said. "But I want a full rundown on everything we know about that asshole Leo."

"I doubt it would be him," Dave said. "He wouldn't have known that she was here. Unless you started to make inquiries, but he couldn't have gotten here that fast."

"No, but a couple days ago we had a cell phone brought over, and that's when I called you," he said. "The islanders have known I was here but only started showing interest more recently, after I was up and around."

"It's possible that word got out to the big world now that you are finally well enough to be recognizable."

"She kept me pretty isolated for a long time," he said. "And I owe her for that too. Because she gave me that time frame, that window, to get better."

"We'll find her," Dave said, and the surety in his voice was something hard to argue with.

And knowing that his buddy was rarely wrong, Bullard allowed some of Dave's calmness and strength to settle into his soul. Bullard reached up and stretched his neck and his back. "I can't believe how long I've been out," he muttered. "I feel like I'm way behind and desperate to get up to speed."

"We can't believe you're actually here," he said, with a smile. "It seems like we've been looking for you forever."

"Well, here I am," he said, "and apparently I brought trouble where it shouldn't have been."

"Come on. You can't blame yourself for this, even if it does go clear back to the airplane crash," he said. "Remember. We still have to find out who is ultimately behind all this."

"I can't imagine there are all that many options," he said. "Have I been such an asshole?"

"No, but you've put away a lot of people," he said. "And we have to remember that."

"Maybe," he said. "It still seems like I didn't do anything to deserve all this."

"Hell yes, you did," Dave said, with a hard laugh. "Think of all the governments happy for your assistance, and of all the people who have been very unhappy to feel the reach of you and your team."

Bullard looked at his friend with a lopsided grin. "I guess. In the criminal world, they don't take responsibility for their actions, do they?"

"Nope. And they're not starting now either. Don't ever think that this wasn't something that could have ever happened because honestly, revenge has always been in the cards."

"I guess, but it's pretty damn shitty when it's not me who's been taken but her."

"In the criminal mind, you're the one who brought this on by surviving the plane crash," he said. "Yet you know that you've been given a second chance. It's up to you to decide what you want to make of it."

"That sounds like some heebie-jeebie bullshit New Age stuff," he muttered.

"Ah, but it's the truth, and you know it."

"Doesn't mean I want to listen."

"Hell," Dave said, feigning disgust, "you don't listen in the best of times."

Bullard burst out laughing at that. "You have a point there."

"I know you really well," Dave said. "No way in hell you would be anything other than yourself, and I'm so grateful that, even after all you've been through, I can still see you being you."

"Ditto," he said. "But now let's make sure that whoever it is who's taken her pays the price for being them."

CHAPTER 9

WHEN SHE AND her kidnapper finally reached the mainland, Leia was almost numb. Her body was sloshed with water, and she could barely even talk. Her teeth chattered, and, even though a hot sun baked down on her, she hadn't had enough time to dry out. She was quickly picked up and tossed over his shoulder, and he stepped out onto a small marina. Nobody cared or appeared to even notice that she was being carted off in this way. He quickly slipped her off his shoulder and carried her, as if she were a damsel in distress.

Which she definitely was, but he was the one reason for her state. And because she couldn't do anything, and the grip that he had her in was like iron, she didn't even struggle. She was so damn weak and cold that she couldn't cry out either. She just glared up at her kidnapper.

He smiled. "Not exactly how you thought the day would end, is it?" he said cheerfully.

"I don't know if you're prepared for the way *your* day will end," she said, through her chattering teeth.

"Man, you're cold, aren't you? I hate to even pick you up and carry you, you're so icy."

She said, "You left me getting pounded by water."

He shrugged. "Wasn't really expecting you to get that cold. If you get sick, I won't be happy."

"Then you need to get me warm," she muttered. But her body now convulsed with shivers.

He looked at her in concern. "You're no good to me if you're dead."

She gave a broken laugh. "You haven't even told me why you've taken me."

"Well," he said, "I am putting you up between two bidders."

She stared up at him, her eyes going wide. "What?"

"Well, when we—when word got out to the real world that somebody named Bullard might have survived the crash, there was definitely some interest. I heard about a bunch of guys trying to take out Bullard's team, but I'd been off on the sidelines, until I was contacted by somebody else who wanted to make sure that now that they'd discovered you, that you stayed quiet."

She stared at him in shock. "So this is about me?"

"See? That's the thing about people. They always think it's about them." Then he laughed and laughed and laughed. "It is about you," he said. "I'm just trying to figure out how to cash in on a double set of profits here."

"And that is?"

"Well, by kidnapping you, I'm pretty well guaranteeing that Bullard's coming too. Coming after me. But the way I see it, then I can get paid for you, and I can get paid for him," he said. "And then I can just disappear."

She stared up at him, shocked at his audacity, and yet it made a sick kind of sense. "Do you really think you'll survive him?"

"He's not so tough," he said, "and he did get brought down on the plane after all."

"Doesn't mean he'd be fooled a second time." Even

though she had no idea what the initial circumstances were that had brought down Bullard, she couldn't imagine that he'd get onto any plane again easily. But then again it was Bullard, so who knew? He seemed to take risks all the time to have ended up in such a mess and having nightmares about all the violence in his world. "He's a good man," she said. "You've got no business setting him up for a murder."

"I didn't say anything about murder. I don't know anything about a murder," he said, with that false innocence in his tone. "Why this guy wants Bullard has nothing to do with me."

"Do you know who it is?"

"Yep, I sure do," he said. "It's kinda funny actually. Somebody else is looking to set up a business and take over Bullard's spot in the hierarchy. Especially now that Kingdom Securities is circling the drain."

She remembered hearing that name. "Did you have anything to do with them going down?"

"Hell no," he said. "That woman was sheer poison. You only get involved with somebody like that if you don't want to live very long."

She frowned, trying to piece together the bits, but it wasn't easy. Finally she just asked, "Who is it who wants Bullard dead?"

"Well, this guy does, and he's willing to pay big money."

"And are you the only one after Bullard?"

"Well, I would have said yes, but I don't trust this guy either, so, probably not. I'll have to prove Bullard's existence and make sure I'm the one who gets the payout."

"Wow," she said, "who knew this world was so cutthroat?"

"Absolutely no honor among thieves," he said, "and anybody who tells you otherwise is a liar."

"Good to know," she muttered. "Not that I expect to spend any time with thieves."

"Ha! Some people would say that Bullard was the worst of the worst."

"No," she said quietly, "that I know is a lie. But go ahead and tell yourself whatever you need to in order to justify sending this innocent man to his death."

He laughed. "God, when a woman falls in love," he said, "it's such a joke."

"What's the matter? Did nobody ever love you?" she asked, with a pitying voice.

He glared at her. "I can have any fucking woman I want."

"Well, you can probably have sex with any woman. But only if she's getting something out of it," she corrected. His jaw stiffened, and he didn't say another word. She realized that she probably shouldn't piss him off quite so much, but it was a little hard not to when she was his prisoner and freezing to boot. When he stepped on board another boat that looked like a small yacht, she was carried downstairs and tossed onto a bed, a bunch of blankets thrown on top of her.

He cut her ties. "Now make sure you dry out and keep yourself alive. You're of absolutely no use to me otherwise," he said. "And, if you'll continue to be so mouthy, remember that I'd just as soon put a bullet in your head and walk away. Your choice."

With that, he slammed the door, sealing her in. She quickly grabbed the blankets and rubbed her arms, slowly at first because her hands were uncoordinated and her arms didn't seem to have the strength to make anything move. But finally she got some blood circulating, and then she kept it up, with more and more rubbing, more pinching and slapping of her skin, all in order to make the blood circulate better and stronger.

Her teeth still chattered in fits and starts. It would be really bad at times, and then they would calm down for a while, and then start up really bad again. But over time she felt that she was slowly winning the war. When she could finally stop with the rubbing, she wrapped the blankets around her, curled up, still shivering every once in a while, but almost back up to her normal body temperature.

She felt herself lulled into a deep sleep from the exhaustion of the cold. She was petrified to fall asleep in case he came down when she was out, but she didn't have much choice. She needed her energy in order to find that moment when she could get free of this asshole. Right now she didn't have too many options. At least it didn't appear that way.

She knew that, for somebody like Bullard, this place was probably full of weapons options, but she wasn't trained like he was. She'd been trained to heal and to save people, not to kill them. And, for the first time ever in her life, she was wondering about changing her stance on that. Because, if she had a scalpel in her hand right now, she'd have taken this kidnapping asshole's life in a heartbeat.

"KANO JUST CONFIRMED that they're talking to the islanders," Dave said.

Bullard turned to look at him in shock. "He got to the island that fast?"

"He flew over in a seaplane," he said.

"Is that even possible?"

"He knew somebody who gave him a lift. He's on the

island doing a quick check. He said there's no sign of her, and nobody's seen her."

"Which means our best bet is the asshole out here in front of us."

"After he talks to a couple more people, Kano's getting back on the seaplane. A witch doctor here is looking for, … has been waiting for Terk."

At that, Bullard straightened, turned to look at him, and said, "Oh my God, that old seer woman, the medicine woman on the island. She's been talking about Terk finding me."

"Good," Dave said, "because that's who sent me here."

"Damn! I forgot all about that," he said. "I did get the message earlier, but it didn't make any sense to me. I didn't remember who he was."

"Well, Terk's damn hard to forget," Dave muttered.

"You're not kidding there. So he really found me? Jesus."

Dave shook his head at that. "That guy's a genius."

"No, I'd say he's driven by whatever it is that powers that craziness in his head. He's psychic, and there's absolutely no explanation for it. Either you believe or you don't."

"Well, I'll tell you this," Dave said. "He's the one who sent me out this way to begin with, and, when I would turn around to head back, he stopped me."

"He called and stopped you?"

"He finally did, after I wouldn't listen." His tone turned softer.

Bullard started to laugh. "God, that sounds like him too."

"And when I got him on the phone, he was pretty frustrated that I wasn't listening to him."

"And had you actually heard him? Like speaking into

your brain?"

Dave was quiet for a long moment, and then he said, "Yes. I did. But I didn't believe it. I thought I had to be mistaken, that I was just dreaming things up because I wanted to."

"Yeah, he's, … he's good at that," Bullard said. "I bet he gave you shit afterward, didn't he?"

"Yeah, he sure did," Dave said, shaking his head. "Believe me. At this point in time, I'm a firm believer. Terk was pretty sad and said that the bulk of the world has to have a hands-on experience like this in order to become a believer. He was pretty fed up with trying to convince those who he needed to act to listen to him."

"I imagine that would be pretty frustrating," Bullard said, his gaze on the approaching horizon. "What the hell will we do here? We'll never find her."

"We'll find her."

Just then they heard a plane flying overhead. As it did, it dipped its wings. Bullard raised a hand, as somebody waved down at him. "Jesus Christ," he said, his heart filling with joy. "It'll be good to see everybody again."

"You have no idea," Dave said, shaking his head.

"I just want to go home and hide away." Then he stopped abruptly and looked at Dave. "That's what she would say too, isn't it?"

"Again you get to reevaluate what you want to do and how you want to do it now," he said. "No need for you to go out on missions. No need for you to go out and prove that you're the big bwana."

"Is that what I was doing?" he asked in a dry tone.

"Some of the time I think you were, yes," Dave muttered.

"Maybe, but that seems simplistic."

"Sure it is. You were looking for yourself. Yet it took something like this for you to stop and to figure out who you actually are."

"Maybe. The whole thing's pretty insane."

"It is. So let's find her and get you guys home again."

"Let's get all of us home," he said.

"That's for sure. Everybody's had more than enough of this shit for a while."

"I can imagine."

"They've all grown through the experience though," he said. "Almost all of them have found partners along the way, too."

Bullard stared at him and shook his head. "That doesn't sound like my guys."

"I think they got a pinch of Levi's fairy dust," Dave said in a dry tone.

"I don't know," he said. "What about you? Did you get it too?"

Dave shook his head. "Not me," he said. "I'm still as single as ever."

"Not sure that's a good thing," he said. "I'm starting to feel pretty old and broken myself."

"Yeah, and maybe that's to be expected, considering all you've been through. It goes back to that thing about you getting to choose who and what you want to be from now on, remember?"

"Remind me of that when it's all over," he said, "because right now it doesn't seem like it's even possible. Not while assholes are out there trying to steal a beautiful woman like Leia."

"The question is, why?"

As soon as they pulled up close to the marina, Bullard looked around and said, "Jesus, boats are everywhere. How will we find her?"

"I know, but don't forget. We've got satellite, and we've got people helping us." Sure enough, seconds later his phone rang, and they were given instructions where to pull up. They had to change marinas and go down the coast a bit.

"But we don't even know where she is," Bullard cried out, frustrated.

"The team is casing the entire shoreline here," Dave assured him, "looking for the boat."

"And that won't be enough," Bullard said, staring at him. "We were supposed to catch them before they got here."

"We were hoping to, but we didn't. Now we have to find them."

"And that's like hunting a needle in a haystack." His frustration started to overwhelm him. But he pulled back, knowing he needed a clear head to help save her. And save her was exactly what he planned to do. As soon as he hopped out onto the pier, a group of men walked toward him. His land legs were not quite there yet, and he was a little stiff, but, as soon as he saw Ryland, he just stared. "Dear God," he said, "I didn't think there was any way you would survive."

Ryland wrapped him up in a gentle hug, elated to see his friend. Two great big bear-size men, rejoicing, since the last time they'd seen each other, free-falling from the sky. "Ditto," Ryland said, staring at him, his hands reaching out as he studied Bullard. "It looks like you took the worst of it."

"Yeah, it was a pretty rough ride for a while," he said, "and I'm not sure even yet how close I am to being where I need to be, but I'm a hell of a lot better than I was. At least I know who you are."

"So what's this about the missing woman who saved you?"

"She was kidnapped, not even two hours ago. They took off by boat," he said. Just then came Fallon first, with Kano there and Garret. A large part of his main team, something he never thought he'd see. Wrapping him up, the three of them, gentle and careful, shared the moment.

"Any progress?" Bullard asked them, right back to business.

"We've been hunting up and down the shore," Ryland said, "Only one person so far has admitted to seeing the boat come in, and he clammed up immediately."

"Are you pressuring him?"

"Already have," he said, "the pressure was money."

"It almost always is," he said bitterly. "And what did you pry loose?"

"He didn't see clearly, but he saw the woman put onto another boat. Her kidnapper was carrying her, as if she were injured."

"That would be her probably," he said, "although she wasn't injured."

"He wondered because she wasn't fighting."

"Maybe she couldn't," Bullard said.

"That's what I wondered too."

"Did he see where they went?"

"He says he didn't. He looked away and was talking to somebody else, and then they were gone. But he was staring out of the marina, and nobody left that way. So as far as he's concerned, she's still here."

Bullard stared at him in shock. "Here?" he said, as he spun around, looking at what had to be hundreds of boats.

"Yeah," Fallon said, "right here."

"We're about to set up a search," Ryland said.

"Do we need any legal authority in any of this?" Dave asked.

"I don't think anybody gives a shit," Kano said. "Now that we've got Bullard back—but you're not free and clear yet, it seems."

"No, I'm sure as hell not," he said. "That woman saved my life, and I can do no less than to help her now."

"We understand," Dave said. "We've got this." Then he went on to fill them in on some of her history and the conversation they'd had with Ice. Everybody's faces turned grim as they realized this had happened to her in the United States, a place that most people didn't associate with these kinds of things.

"It's too unbelievable," Kano said. "And yet it's not."

"Right." They split up and started a boat-by-boat search. Several men weren't allowed to get on some of the boats; others went on regardless. And they continued with a mass search, intent to search every single boat, if they had to.

Bullard knew that the authorities would quickly step in and stop them if they caused too much of a ruckus, though it was a pretty wild area of town anyway, from the looks of it. A yacht club farther down was much more high-end. The type of place he would expect the authorities to be called in on if they bulldozed their way onboard. But he would do it anyway, if that's what it took.

As the men went from boat to boat, they asked questions, searching for the woman who'd been carried off of one boat and onto another one. Finally they heard a shout from Garret. Bullard hobbled his way down, feeling the passage of time in constant action without the rest that he had become accustomed to. And, sure enough, Garret was with another man.

"This guy saw him."

Immediately all attention turned to the wizened old man, who sat at the side of a fishing boat.

"What did you see?"

He pointed to an empty berth. "They were in there. Then he left for a time, came back at a dead run, untied, and took off down the coast."

"Did you hear him say where he was going?"

"No, there was an argument with a female, but he wasn't too worried. He just hopped in, untied, and left."

"Have you seen him before?"

"Nope, I haven't seen him, but I do know the boat."

At that, they spun and looked at him again. He shrugged and said, "It belongs down the road a little bit. Not the fancy yacht place, but past that to the fishing village."

"Tell us exactly where it belongs. There's a good chance he's taking it home."

"Maybe, or maybe he's only taking it for a little way," the guy said. "Now, if you want any other information, you'll have to pay for it."

CHAPTER 10

LEIA DIDN'T KNOW how long she had been kept captive down below. But the boat continued to travel for what seemed like hours. When it finally slowed and continued along the coast, she assumed they had gotten in very close to the landmass. Nothing could really go against the current unless it was at full power. Waves washed up against the boat as it gently moved. She wasn't sure if he was trying to hide or trying to find a place to dock. Either would fit the scenario, just because this guy was such an asshole. She didn't really want to consider that, but, at the same time, all she could think about was a poor decision she'd made.

Since her captor had actually said somebody had wanted her brought in once her name had popped up, all she could think about was the damn surgeon. Leo was just the kind of person to come after her, in case she had said anything to anyone. Making sure that she was dead was one more little thread in his world to be tied off. But it's not like she could do anything about it. She'd hidden for five years, but her mistake was that she hadn't told Bullard why. She had told him a partial truth and had held back important information. And now she had no one to blame but herself.

She swore to herself softly. She had known Bullard and hadn't wanted him to stress, since his healing had been paramount. It was so important that he become that person he so needed to be. He was a grizzly—and a wounded grizzly for the longest time. Now, as he reared his head and pulled that massive body of his back into a healthy active male, he'd also become a moving target.

As she lay here, she wondered just how much that stupid doctor was doing here. When the door opened, she confronted her kidnapper. "So why does the doctor want me? Why not just have me killed?"

He looked at her in surprise, then shrugged. "I presume he wants something from you."

"I don't have anything to give him."

"Well, he seems to think otherwise," her kidnapper said calmly. "Look. I don't give a shit. I don't ask questions, and, when I get a directive, I follow it. The money is too good to pass up."

She nodded. "Of course it is. And you don't care at all that he's killed several people on his table."

"Hey, I'm sure even the best surgeons lose a certain portion of their patients anyway."

"Oh, they do," she said, hating that he was confirming the surgeon's role in all this. "The problem is that these are people he killed on purpose."

He looked at her in surprise and then laughed. "Isn't that the way of it?" he said. "So very typical of the world."

"Yes," she said. "Just not very nice."

"Maybe not, but it is what it is."

She groaned. "I don't know what he thinks he wants from me."

"Well, if you saw him do something, he probably wants to know who you told. So he can kill them too." With that, he flashed her a bright grin, then turned and walked back up to the top of the deck.

She lay curled up in bed, wondering if that's exactly what it was.

It made sense in a way. Leo couldn't know about what else she had done, could he? She'd forgotten about it, but she had tossed the flash drive into the safe deposit box at the bank and had quickly disappeared. At the time everybody else had expected her to disappear, so they were just damn grateful when she had quietly slipped away. She hadn't thought that he was following her back then.

But, of course, once Bullard's people found out Bullard was alive and that she was the one who had saved him, they had likely made inquiries. Once that happened, it probably got back to the surgeon and his cronies, which ultimately led to this. She wondered who on the damn island she could thank for assisting. But then, no point in blaming them. They lived a very poor life, and, of course, she should have expected them to be susceptible to offers of money for information.

Then there was the old seer woman. Leia didn't have a clue what her role in all this was, if she had played one. She seemed to be a messenger for whoever this Terk person was, and that made no sense either.

Groaning, Leia curled up under the blankets once again. She could use food and doubted there would be any coming her way, though water would also be nice and more important.

She lay here wondering, wishing she had a way to communicate. But she had always been one to drop the cell phones off the deep end and had done so after her world had been blown up and she had moved to the island. Getting Bullard that phone had started it all, bringing the questions and the islanders over. Ultimately it had brought enemies she had no idea she'd even had. Although realistically, Terk knew Bullard was there long before she'd asked for a cell phone, so something probably would have happened anyway.

Now what the hell was she supposed to do?

When her kidnapper eventually came back down, he gave her a bowl with several pieces of fruit and a bottle of water. She sat up and took a big slug of water, then gratefully reached for the piece of fruit closest to her. "I wasn't sure if you would feed me," she confessed.

"You need to be in good health when I hand you over," he said. "And I have to be just far enough ahead of the second half of my payout but not so far that they can't catch up."

"Wait! What's going on?" She froze, and her gaze shot up to stare at him.

He laughed. "Did you really think I didn't know we were being followed?"

Her gaze went to the tiny window on the far side. She didn't see anything the one time she had looked out.

"They were doing pretty good too," he said, "but I'd have expected more from somebody like Bullard."

Her breath sucked in and out of her chest at that. "And yet you'll hand him over to be killed," she said, striving for calmness, though inside her heart was breaking.

"You bet I will," he said. "He's worth big money. Bullard is the symbol of a deal gone wrong on many layers. So this guy just wants to take Bullard out once and for all."

"Okay," she said quietly. "But wasn't that the end result already?"

"It was the intent," he said, "but his body wasn't found, so his demise couldn't be confirmed. Bullard survived and so did the rest of his team, even though many attempts were made, and many mercenaries were hired and lost. At the end of the day, they all did a better job than the ones this guy had hired."

"Bullard's men did a better job?" She was trying desperately to get through the kidnapper's convoluted information.

"That's what I just said," he barked, with a snort. "Bloody women," he said. "Give them an ounce of brains, and they think they know everything."

She pinched the bridge of her nose, wondering what else she could ask. "Do you know anything about the doctor who put the price on my head?"

"Nope. Just that the money has been verified."

"That's important too," she said. "So you'll just hand me over to him? Or to a third party?"

"Third party. Always a third party," he said. "Don't want to take the chance of somebody going back on their deal. If I didn't get paid, he doesn't get you."

"And, of course, if the deal goes sour, you kill me, so he can't get what he wants either," she said.

"Now you're getting it," he said, with a broad smile. "But as long as you're alive and the money deal is happening, then you'll be safe with me." And, with that, he turned and walked out.

WHEN THE OLD man was paid, he quickly provided the location where the boat belonged. By then, Fallon had already pulled up with a boat he'd rented. A heavy power-boat, with a powerful engine on the back, room for all of them, and, if Bullard wasn't mistaken, full weaponry on the inside. Bullard slapped Fallon on the shoulder as he walked on board. "Good man," he muttered.

Fallon shook his head. "Like anything else would be acceptable."

"Yeah, I guess I'm a bit of a hard-ass, aren't I?" Bullard wondered.

"You think?" Fallon said, but then he grinned. "Damn good to see you."

"You too. And I'll be safe to talk to once we find her," he said.

"She means that much to you?" Fallon could tell something was in Bullard's voice.

Bullard looked at him and smiled. "Yeah. Nothing like a few months on a deserted island to change your perspective on life."

Fallon nodded slowly. "That's good to hear."

Neither had to say any more because Bullard knew; they all did. But it was suddenly a different world out there, and he didn't want to go forward without Leia at his side. Though there had been many events in his life where he'd been forced to deal with circumstances he didn't want anything to do with. But no way he would let her be hurt.

Just then Dave came running down the boardwalk. He'd been on the phone. "So," he said, "I've just heard from a source that somebody was interested when the news came out that you were alive. There was also interest in who might have rescued you, and the information included something about a New York doctor who'd been in hiding for five years."

"She hasn't been in hiding," he said, "not in the sense of hiding away from law enforcement or anything. She's been hiding from life."

"Well, apparently somebody put a price on her head."

At that, Bullard stopped and stared, fury building in his chest. "That'll be that damn doctor," he said instantly.

"That's my take on it," Dave said. "We're getting as much information as we can right now." He hopped onto the boat, and the two of them took seats at the back. Fallon stepped up to stand beside Dave while Ryland took the wheel, and in no time they were underway.

As they sped across the water, Bullard completely ignored the beautiful blue sky in this tropical paradise. He'd been living here for months now, and it's not like he ever wanted to be complacent about it, but it was really hard to see anything but the evil patterns weaving around them. "So this guy was keeping an eye out for her, and, now that she's surfaced, he wants, what? To talk to her? If the goal was just to kill her, they could have taken care of that on the island."

"That's what I was wondering," Fallon said. "Unless he thinks she's told somebody or she has some proof or something."

"I don't know," Bullard said. "We never really talked about it."

"Is she the kind who might do something like that?"

He tilted his head to the side, thinking about her. "She's definitely a survivor, so, in that case, the answer would be yes," he said. "So we'll need to ask her about that when we find her. But a few other questions are on the top of my list."

"Like what?" Fallon asked.

"Like why the hell she didn't expose that bastard at the time," he snapped. "She said that he's killed before. On the operating table for sure, but I wonder if there was more even than that."

"Of course he had a certain amount of—I don't know—leeway, since so many patients in a practice of that nature were probably likely to die anyway," Fallon said.

"Potentially, but that would be pretty harsh to just assume that a percentage of the patients would die on the table."

Then Dave spoke up. "Remember? A lot of doctors won't take on cases with poor potential for good outcomes. Too many deaths hurt their survival statistics, which impacts the cost of their malpractice coverage."

"If that asshole is putting her through this over something that stupid, I may just kill him myself," Bullard said immediately. "What a horrid world we have become."

"We already knew that," Fallon said, "but now it's a matter of trying to minimize the damage." Bullard nodded, as Fallon went on. "I still think we need more information about the whole scenario with this doctor."

"Ice is working on that," Bullard said. "Her father had some contacts that he would get a hold of, although he is probably in surgery for 90 percent of the day, and we can't wait for that intel to come through."

"I think we can," Dave said. "We'll be at least an hour getting up the coast."

"Well, we better shave off at least ten minutes," he snapped because he couldn't bear the thought of showing up only to find he was ten minutes too late. He sat here, trying desperately to stay focused on what was happening, though his mind was spinning about the doctor. Was this really about Bullard, or was it about Leia? Surely it couldn't be about both of them.

Or could it?

Yet, at the same time, he had suffered, and so had she. He felt terrible in a way since he'd actually taken her out of hiding and brought her back into the real world. He had no idea enemies lay in wait for her, any more than she had for him. Her protectiveness had been as much about her own peace and sanity as his. How awful that they had both ended up as targets. His shoulders were broad, and he'd been a target many times, but it was much harder on her. He just had to find a way to get them both out of here safely.

"Just got a text from Levi," Dave said, holding up his phone. "Ice's father is having a meeting right now with the hospital board members he knows."

"Good," Bullard said in surprise. "Christ, he got on that fast."

"Well, everybody knows we don't have any time to spare right now," Dave said. "Whether the target's you or her, it doesn't matter. You're both in danger, and we won't get to the bottom of this until we actually get whoever it is who's hunting you."

"I was really hoping we would have some answers by now," Bullard said.

"We all did," Fallon said, "but we've checked every person we know of on this earth who would have a grudge against you, yet still somebody has hired these men to take you out."

"So maybe it's somebody that we don't know," Bullard said.

"That would make sense in one way, but there has to be a connection," Fallon said.

"We've deposed a lot of tyrants," Bullard said, "and it doesn't take a big connection to see that some of those guys would be after me."

"But they have to really care about it," Fallon said. "It can't be just about your security company because seriously, if you died, it won't do anything for them."

"It would make them smile, at least," he growled.

"That's true," Dave said, as he stared off in the distance.

"And what if it's somebody that we do know," Fallon said, "but not somebody we would expect?"

"Like an enemy presuming to be a friend?" Dave asked.

"Something like that, yeah," Fallon said, with a nod.

"At this point we have no choice but to look at options like that," Dave said. "Do you have anybody in mind?"

"Not really," Fallon said, "because we're surrounded by a lot of people, but we vet all of them. To think that anybody we vetted is involved would mean our system sucks."

"It doesn't suck," Dave said. "We have one of the best in the world. The problem is, we don't always know what's going on in somebody's mind."

"So we take another look," Bullard said. "As soon as you mentioned Deedee, I was thinking that maybe she would have had something to do with it, or even Michael. But—"

"Not Michael or Deedee, but definitely some employees and ex-employees of theirs went off on their own. But, in the midst of all that, we found out they'd been hired on by this guy, like all the others."

"So somebody who knows me. Somebody close enough to the industry to understand Kingdom Securities. So, after they imploded, a huge gap must have opened up. Has anybody stepped in to fill the gap in the workforce?"

"No," Dave said, "not yet. But I'm sure it won't be long in coming."

CHAPTER 11

L EIA WOKE WITH a start. The boat was gently rocking, but it wasn't moving. They'd stopped. She felt frozen, yet her body was warm. Slowly she shook off the feeling, got up and tiptoed across to look out the window, but all she found on that side was water as far as she could see. Just water. She wanted to send out a warning to Bullard somehow but didn't see a way to do it. It warmed her heart to think he was behind her, yet it terrified her to consider that he was out there and that this guy knew it. Bullard had to know there was a nasty possibility of being caught, but did he know it was actually a trap? And, if he didn't know, how the hell was she supposed to get him a message?

She groaned and slowly sank back down again. She listened intently above, but it didn't sound like anybody was up there. She walked over to the door and stared at it, wondering if she should try to open it up. Anybody in their right mind would try, so surely it couldn't be wrong. Who could blame her for that since it was just human nature? Knowing that, if her kidnapper was around, he would be pissed, she slowly turned the handle. It turned, but, when she went to push, it didn't budge. She'd been locked inside.

Pissed, though she really hadn't been expecting anything different, she stretched out again and stared at the door. How could she get out? What if he didn't come back? What if this guy got into trouble or got himself shot? It's not like he was a model citizen. He could easily have people hunting him too. Even just thinking about the possibility of being trapped here made her cringe.

She studied the door hinges. She might be able to pop them off, but it wouldn't be easy. She wasn't sure any tools or weapons were down here, or anything she could use. She was in a bedroom, not a galley. It was kind of odd in that it looked like it used to be a kitchen area but had been converted to a rough bedroom. She quickly went through a counter and some cupboards, hoping she might find something she could use as a weapon, but, so far, she couldn't find anything. In other words, her kidnapper had done his homework and had stripped it pretty decently. For that she hated him; at the same time, she realized it was foolish to waste the time and energy because this is what he did for a living, so how could she expect him to do anything less.

The fact that she didn't want to be part of his income stream or his plans to set himself up for a future life of leisure wasn't something he gave a shit about. He lived to prey on others, just like Leo, the murdering doctor. That thought just brought her mind back around to that whole damn scenario. If she was handed over to him, what would she do? He'd kill her for sure and wouldn't even think twice about it and would probably smile and look into her eyes as he slashed the artery up her throat. He'd probably like to watch her lifeblood drain away, happy that a thorn in his side was finally gone.

She thought that, just by disappearing, she'd be safe but apparently not. Did he know she had that flash drive? She had never even decided what to do about it, after putting it out of her mind and leaving the country. The tiny device had been an easy thing for her to forget, to safely store away, but apparently he hadn't forgotten, ... if he even knew about it. She didn't want to think he did, but what other conclusion could she come to? This kidnapping asshole was here and preying on her now all because of Leo.

And Bullard.

Damn Bullard for asking for that cell phone and for contacting the world. Yet it wasn't his fault, since he was just trying to get his own life back. He couldn't have known that reaching out to his public life again would have exposed her to the public as well. And who knew that after all this time anybody even gave a damn about her?

She thought for sure the doctor would have died of old age or some disease by now or would have been murdered by somebody who had finally realized what he was doing. But instead he'd apparently been waiting and watching to see where she surfaced, then hadn't wasted any time and had jumped on it. Now she was waiting for him to show his ugly face and decide her fate. And, at that, she grew even more determined to not let him have the outcome he wanted.

Surely she could do something to defend herself. She'd been given blankets. She was pretty damn sure Bullard would find some way to make a weapon out of it. Even if she didn't know what, surely she could create something. She studied the blanket for a long time, then noted a rip along one side. Carefully she tore off a strip and wrapped it around both fists and jerked it hard between her hands. If nothing else, she could wrap that around somebody's throat and strangle them to death.

With a knife, she could do some serious damage. One of the good things about having surgical knowledge was that she knew exactly where to get somebody to make sure they didn't get up and attack her again. But, without anything sharp, she would be limited. With that in her mind, she set to hunting even deeper around the place, checking under the mattress and under the bunk, looking for anything that would give her a better offensive weapon.

When she couldn't find anything, she sat down, completely unnerved to think that this guy had managed to lock her in a prison bereft of anything she could use to defend herself. When she heard footsteps on the deck above, she froze and sat down, pulling a blanket against her. She kept the rope tied around her one hand, just in case. But he walked slow and steady, pacing above. She wasn't sure what he was after or why he was even up there, but he didn't appear to care about her down below.

She wondered if she should pound on the door and cry out. What if it wasn't him though? What if it was somebody else, … somebody who was after her? With all these thoughts going around in her head, she worried that she'd alert the wrong person. In this case, the devil she knew might be better than the devil she didn't. But then the other part of her brain kicked in.

What if it's Bullard? But if it was Bullard, he would completely destroy the boat to find her, and she knew that. He would tear apart the boat piece by piece to find her. So not Bullard up there. That was an easy answer. But who the hell was it? When the footsteps stopped, she realized an opportunity had just fallen through her fingers. And she swore.

The boat had rocked a little as the man had gotten on and off, so she wasn't sure if another boat had pulled beside them or what. But she couldn't see out since the other side of the window had been boarded over. That made her jump, wondering if it had been broken. Because *broken* meant *glass*. She quickly raced to the plywood, and, using her fingers, she tried to pry off one of the boards. She had almost got it off when she became aware of footsteps again.

She froze and quickly sat back down, holding the blanket wrapped around her. This time the door between them opened, but she could tell that he had first removed something he had placed against it. She couldn't get that door open because he'd probably weighted it down so she couldn't budge it, keeping her securely locked in. When he came down and looked at her, he smiled, and said. "Good, you're awake."

"What's good about it?" she muttered.

"Well, there's food for you," he said. "Not that it's much, but it'll keep you alive. He dropped a bowl of what looked like rice and maybe vegetables.

"How much longer are you keeping me?"

"Well, I've got to take some pictures to verify that it's you," he said. "And, once that's been verified, I'll set up a meeting with the third party."

"And then they'll be responsible for handing me over to the doctor?"

"Yep, that's how it works," he said.

"But doesn't that mean you'll lose a portion of your money to the third party?"

"Sure I will," he said. "But you've got to figure that somebody out there has to be trusted. Otherwise you'll never make the deal happen."

"So they get to make money off the fact that you did all the work," she pressed.

He shrugged and said, "Yeah, it sucks, doesn't it?"

"Big-time," she said, "but you don't care, so whatever."

"Well, I do care," he said, "but it's not like I can do anything about it."

She just nodded and didn't say anything, but she was hoping he would pick up on what she was trying to do, which was put some doubt in his mind about making the deal happen this way. It was one thing to deal with him, but another thing entirely to deal with a third party whose only interest was an exchange. They would get money off the top if the deal went through, and they would lose money if it didn't. That didn't sound like a deal she wanted to be part of at all, but there was only so much she could do.

He pointed to the food. "If you don't want that, I'll take it away."

She immediately reached out from under the blanket for the bowl and snatched it up.

He laughed and said, "I should keep somebody as a pet," he said. "You're quite entertaining."

And, with that, he turned walked away, going back up the stairs again. She listened when he snapped the door shut, but he didn't lock it or put the weight back against it again. She would count that as a success. If she could keep him slightly off center and not thinking she was any kind of a threat, then maybe she'd get a chance to escape.

If nothing else, she might get up top and dive off. They had to be close enough to something to give her a shot at escaping. She was a hell of a swimmer but maybe not for the open ocean. Still, she was pretty damn sure she'd rather drown than become another man's *pet*. And, in this case, she'd was on the way to becoming another man's purchase, which sounded just as bad and was probably worse.

The doctor had no interest in keeping her alive; he probably just wanted to find out what she had and who she had told. And, if she didn't give him the answers, he would just kill her. Why would he worry about niceties like trying to keep her alive? If she didn't have anything of value, she'd just become someone to cause him more trouble. She was surprised he was even doing this much, but considering she did have a thumb drive, maybe it wasn't so surprising after all.

Now she had to wonder if she could contact anyone to give that flash drive to who would see justice was done after she was long gone. Surely somebody out there gave a damn. If not for her, how about patients Leo had already killed, yet nobody knew about? And, if she couldn't get that flash drive to somebody who could do something with it, nobody would ever know. And that she couldn't allow to happen.

"DO WE HAVE an aerial view yet?" Bullard asked anybody, as Ryland expertly handled the speedboat on the water, even at full throttle.

"Kano is in the air," Fallon said, studying his phone. "He's in a small float plane, searching the area."

"Good," Bullard said, with a note of satisfaction. "That's exactly what we want."

"There's also been mention of a third party involved," Dave said, studying some information that just came in on his phone.

"Look at us," Bullard said. "All we're doing is digital now."

"It's the world we live in," Fallon said. "We would knock on doors if we had any doors to knock on. But, right now, it's all about what's on the dark web, who's buying and who's selling."

"And is somebody buying her or me?"

"Well, we already know there's a price on your head," Fallon said. "There's still a price on all of us actually."

"Which seriously sucks," Bullard said, "because, by having me around, we're getting too many of us in one place, so they can take us all out again."

"Which is what they tried last time," Fallon said, and he looked up to where Ryland was piloting the boat. "But we don't kill so easy."

"No, but we took a hell of a hard beating," he muttered, "and we're damn lucky we all came out of these past few months alive." Shifting his huge body on the bench, they knew better than to ask if he was okay, since he would glare and bite their heads off anyway.

"There is talk about the doctor having recently come under questioning for another death," Dave said, just as his phone rang. "Ice, is that you?"

"It is," she said, "but the connection is really horrible."

"We're at sea, following a boat we're hoping Leia's being held in. I'm putting you on Speaker, so Bullard can hear."

"Good," she said. "Let me fill you in on a little bit that my father managed to find out. So, this doctor," she said, "we'll call him Dr. Smitten, has recently had another high-profile death. One of the surgical nurses suggested that he was at fault and could have saved the patient. She has since been sacked and is screaming."

"Of course she is," he said. "Anything to do with Leia?"

"It was pretty hard to get anybody to talk apparently. Even Dad's friend was not very willing to open up about it. He said it was a raw deal, and she was basically a scapegoat. He said he wouldn't be at all surprised if the surgeon had indeed killed the guy and had blamed her."

"But nobody looked into it?" Dave asked.

"No. There wasn't a whole lot they could do," she said. "Besides, the patient was dead, and the family had been big donors. They were looking for a fast answer and weren't too concerned about whether it was the right one or not."

"Was the death convenient for anybody?" Bullard asked. There was a slight pause while Ice understood the potential implications.

"You know what? I think we'll take a closer look at that," she said, "because another endowment was given to the hospital by the family afterward, which some people thought was a little odd. They took it as a goodwill gesture, understanding that they had worked hard to remove the guilty party, namely Leia in this instance, so their trust had been reconfirmed."

"Or the doctor took out the patient so the living heirs could get whatever money they were looking for, and it was all cleaned up nice and tidy without any nasty media coverage," Bullard said.

"Quite right," Ice said, her voice thoughtful as she considered it. "I think that's a valid point. Might be a little hard to prove though."

"Maybe not," he said. "It's also come to my attention everybody on my team has apparently been on a hit list."

"Yes," she said, her tone dry. "So far, you've been out-foxing them all."

"Thank God. Listen, Ice. Do you guys have any man-power to spare?"

"Always for you," she said. "What do you need from us?"

"A full investigation into that doctor. His background and everything you can dredge up that we can use against him. The hospital, the family of the patient who basically killed Leia's career," he said, "and—"

"Any other suspicious deaths," she said. "It wasn't the first time he's done this. My father's contact implied the same thing. Apparently this guy has quite a mercurial track record. Sometimes he's brilliant, but sometimes, with no rhyme or reason, his patients just up and died from accidents in the operating room."

"Maybe like a ruptured artery that somehow didn't rupture on its own?" Bullard asked.

"Exactly," she said. "Now that I've brought it up to my father, he's quite alarmed that this loose cannon is out there."

"I'm actually more concerned that he could be a paid assassin," he said. "When you think about it, it wouldn't take much for someone in that position to kill off whatever patient needed to go."

"No, it wouldn't," she said. "And we've certainly seen our share of killers doing things for plenty of reasons."

"In this case, I'm wondering if he does it for the thrill, getting away with it under the eye of all these respected doctors and assistants," he said. "Like that nurse who's just raised a hullabaloo. I'd say her life is in danger."

"I'll see if we can track her down," Ice said, "and talk to her ourselves."

"And you better do it quick before somebody decides she's dead weight and needs to go," he said, before ending the call. He looked at Dave. "A killer doctor? What do you think?"

"Unfortunately there's a whole niche market of various assassins these days," he said. "But not normally for pay because they're a bunch of sick bastards, yet why not? If it's something he enjoys and is doing anyway, why not get paid for it at the same time? I'm sure some very grateful and wealthy heirs out there want access to their inheritance but need dear old dad to die first."

"Yeah, I think you're probably right," he said. "With help from Ice and Levi, we've got people on that angle," he said, "so what we have to do is focus on finding Leia."

Just then Fallon turned and called back, "We're coming up on the location."

Immediately Bullard made his way forward and sat down in the co-pilot seat. He looked around at the boats and shook his head. "She could be anywhere."

"I know," Ryland said. "We need to find somebody who's been watching for new arrivals."

"But, in a fishing village like this," he said, "they won't have any registration or check-ins, so we'll have to stop and talk to the locals."

"Not a problem," Fallon said. He motioned up at one of the small piers, where a group of people were gathered, and said, "Drop me off there, Ryland. I'll give you a call when to pick me up again." At that, he prepared to hop out, but Bullard didn't want him to go alone, so Garret ended up getting off with him.

Dropping off the two men, Ryland pulled the boat around, as Bullard said, "I think we should check the boats on the edges. I can't see him pulling right into the middle of things."

"That makes sense," Ryland replied, as they all gazed around, wondering at what point in time they might actually find a fishing boat that held a woman who was likely either unconscious or being held captive belowdeck.

"Would she scream out?" Dave asked.

"Only once," Bullard said. "This guy would take her out in a second if she makes a noise to bring trouble down on him."

"Good point," Dave replied. "Any idea if she has any self-defense skills?"

"I don't know," Bullard said, "but I doubt it." Just then he pointed out a large boat set a little farther back from the others. They drifted toward it, but they saw no sign of anybody on it. "Take some photos," he said, "and see if we can find anybody to recognize who owns it. We need that old guy from the marina," he said.

"I've got his number," Dave said. "That old fisherman's grandson had a phone."

Bullard looked at him in surprise. "I guess in this corner of the world, most people still don't have phones, do they?"

"Nope, just the younger generation," Dave muttered. He took a picture of the boat and sent it to the grandson, along with a message. "Now we have to wait though," he said. They drifted back toward the shore again, seeing if anybody else was of interest. They took photos of a couple other boats, but nothing appeared to be half as interesting as that first old boat. By the time they made it back to where they had dropped off Fallon and Garret, the grandson got back to them.

It wasn't the same boat.

"Of course not," Bullard muttered. "So, who the hell would know where the boat is?" As they drifted closer, he pointed out another handful similar to the one they'd taken a photo of. "What about these?"

"I don't know," Dave said. "It's easy enough to send photos though," which he did. By the time they'd sent half a dozen photos, they got a call from Garret.

"A boat over here on this side," he said, "arrived about twenty minutes ago. One man got off but no woman."

"Any chance she's in there still?"

"I'll make our way over there and check it out," he said.

"It'll be a trap if she's still there," Bullard warned Garret.

"I know," he said. "I'll be waiting for it."

They too moved quietly in the direction of the boat, their engine at a slow idle as they barely moved forward. Bullard saw Garret walking toward the boat in question, getting in position. Maybe forty or fifty boats were here, and men were all over the boats, the docks, and the shore. Some were just sitting around, smoking; others were working on nets, cleaning boats, or bringing in their catch. But this one boat just sat there. They motored ever closer, and Garret came up from the water on their side and slid into the boat. He did it smooth and strong.

"It was touch-and-go for quite a while with him," Dave said. "It's really good to see that he's recovered so well. They all have really."

"Yeah," Bullard said, his voice choking up. "Even me."

"We'll get her back," Dave said. "I promise."

"I know we will," Bullard said. "But until I actually have her safe—" He watched, his throat tight as Garret moved around on the boat checking out the surface, but staying low in case anybody from the shore was watching, which was highly likely. Then he disappeared from sight, and Bullard guessed he'd gone down below. Soon he came back out and slipped back into the water. Bullard's heart sank. "She's not there, is she?"

"Doesn't look like it," Dave said, "but she has to be here somewhere. He's got to be hiding her somewhere nearby."

"Close, but not too close," Bullard said, looking around.

"There's got to be another set of boats, another dock area, or he's just under the trees a little bit." They kept moving, sliding down the coast a little bit farther, before turning around and coming up even closer along the edge.

One boat floated against a dock. It was at the end of the dock, which was pretty rough and tumble. He looked at it, then at Dave. "I want to check that one out."

"That works," Dave said. "We should go pick up Fallon and Garret first," but, even as he looked back, he saw the men coming down the shoreline. When they saw the boat in question, they immediately headed for it at a faster pace but casually, so they didn't attract attention.

Bullard watched carefully from a distance, knowing his crew would do everything they could to keep him from getting into the action too fast, but he desperately wanted to find Leia, and, if that meant getting out there and searching these boats himself, he would do it in a heartbeat. When they came out and shook their heads, Ryland brought their boat closer and picked them up.

"No sign of her," Garret said. "That one boat had a kitchen down below, but nothing like a bed and no sign of a woman having been there."

"Crap. Did anybody on shore have anything to say?"

"No, except that one of the fishermen died this morning."

"What happened to his boat?"

"Turns out his boat is missing," he said in that dry tone.

"Any idea what it looked like?" Dave asked.

"Yeah, exactly like the one we're chasing."

"Has anybody seen it this morning?" Bullard asked.

Fallon shook his head.

"Shit, so he came from here, and we don't know where

he's gone."

"Exactly."

Bullard felt his heart sinking as he realized that she could be anywhere up and down this coast right now. Just then Fallon heard a cry. He turned, jumped off the boat and walked back up the dock, seeing an old woman sitting there. They waited on the shore as close as they could, while he assisted the old woman back down to their boat.

"She'll need some money," Fallon said. Dave didn't even hesitate, as he pulled out money and handed it to the old woman. "Now, it'll take a bit to translate." Fallon worked on it patiently, then finally turned to them and said, "The man who died—his boat was here, and she said he was killed for the boat."

"So, he didn't die of old age then?" Bullard said.

She shook her head, when she understood the question.

"Did she see who did it?"

Fallon worked on getting answers, and the woman shook her head. Finally Fallon said, "She said it was a white man."

"Sure it was, but she had no idea who though, right?"

"Correct."

"Interesting," he said. "We'll have to do something here to see if we can get a little better answer."

"Good luck," Fallon said. "I don't think she knows that much."

But, as they kept digging, she revealed hearing a noise and the sounds of a fight. Then the man was skulking down to take the boat, but she'd never seen him before. The man who died had been poor, but he'd also had done a lot of deals that he shouldn't have. He was known as somebody who would do anything for money. He was also a drunk. At that, she turned and headed back where she came from.

Bullard immediately said to Fallon, "Go ask her if she's got any idea where this guy was going."

Fallon stopped her at the hill and asked, and she pointed up the way they had come. Then she laughed and said something that immediately got Fallon's attention, and he questioned her a little more. When he got back to the boat, Fallon had a new lead. "She said there was a second man."

"A second man, but she doesn't know anything about him or what?"

"According to her, it was the dead guy's brother," he said.

"So we've got two men to deal with now?" Bullard asked.

"Only one at the boat," Fallon clarified. "The other one left on his own."

"So, where's this brother now?"

"He lives just around here," he said.

"Time to go visit," Bullard said, and, with that, they pulled up to the dock. Bullard got out and stretched his legs. He liked being out in the water as much as the next guy, but getting back on land for a bit would help get his legs to calm down somewhat. Following Fallon, who led the way using the directions he'd been given, they headed up to the house.

As they got closer, they crossed paths with an old man who glared at them. Fallon immediately told him who they were looking for. He shook his head, as if he didn't want to talk to them. But then Dave once again held out money. He frowned, then looked at it, looked from one man to the other. "What do you want with him?"

"We think he kidnapped a woman," Bullard said bluntly.

The man looked at him and nodded. "He did. He was

getting money for her."

"Why?"

"Because he could," the old man said, with a cackle.

"Do you know why somebody wanted this woman?"

"He was being paid to bring her."

"Okay, do you know where the handoff will be?"

The old man shrugged and said, "Back up there a couple miles offshore."

The language barrier was a little bit disruptive to sort out, but Fallon eventually understood that they had a meeting place somewhere in the ocean.

"Do you know how much he was getting paid?" Bullard asked.

"I don't know. It was a third party," he said.

"Of course it was," Bullard said. "Any idea how to find him?"

"No," he said, "and, if you want that woman, you'll have to get her fast, before she goes into the system."

"Are you talking the sex trade?"

"Why else would anybody want a woman?" he asked in surprise.

Bullard realized that's what most people would think, and that's probably what the doctor was hoping for. With that, Bullard nodded, and they headed back to the boat. Fallon stopped for a moment and talked with the old man a bit more, but he quickly caught up.

"I told him I'd pay him if he found out anything else."

"Good," Bullard said. "We really need somebody on our side. Or, if not on our side, at least on our payroll. So far, it seems like everybody out here is just looking after themselves."

"It's the way of the world," Dave said. "We've seen it

time and time again."

"I don't like it," Bullard snapped.

"You never did," Dave said. "You've spent a lifetime helping others, and it really gets your goat when anybody pulls shit like this."

"But why her?" he said, shaking his head.

"Bad luck is what I'd say," Fallon said.

"Leia was at the wrong place at the wrong time," Dave suggested, "and somebody with more power and more money managed to screw her life over pretty good. She didn't know how to fight him, so she did the only thing she could think of to survive, and that was to step out of the fight."

"Still sucks," Bullard said.

At that, Fallon's phone rang, and this time it was Kano. Fallon put his phone on Speaker.

"Two boats are about four nautical miles away, and one and a half or two nautical miles out into the ocean," he said. "I've flown over, but I can't keep going back and forth, or I'll make them nervous."

"I'm not sure making them nervous is a bad thing," Bullard said. "We're already headed that way. Can you see us?"

"Yeah, I saw you before," he said. "I'll make another pass and make sure you're on the right course," he said, "then I have to get fuel."

"Good enough," he said. "Stay up as long as you can to make sure we're getting there," he said. "Then go fuel up and park it. Somebody will pick you up."

"Yeah, I'll be glad to set this tank down," he said.

"It's a tank?"

"It sure as hell is," he said, with laugh. "But it flies, so I can't complain."

"Got it," he said. "Let us know when you're down."

"You go find her," he said. "By the way, Bullard. Glad to have you back."

"Me too, thanks," he said, with a big smile, then hung up the phone.

CHAPTER 12

"**W**AKE UP."

A hand roughly grabbed Leia's shoulder and gave her a hard shake. She groaned, and, startled, she scrambled backward on the makeshift bed, staring up at her captor. "What?" she said, brushing her hair off her face.

"It's D-day," he said. "Get yourself upstairs." Looking around, he said, "I'll be glad to be rid of this thing."

"It served your purpose though," she said, trying to stand up.

Grabbing her, he shoved her roughly ahead of him onto the stairs up to the deck. "It did," he said, "but I'm used to much better than this."

"Sorry," she snapped. "I guess kidnappers can't be too picky."

He roared with laughter at that. "You know what? You'd almost be fun to hang around with. It's just that I think women have better purposes, and that is making money," he said, with a sneer.

"Of course you do because you don't have a soul."

"My soul died a long time ago," he said, his voice hard, and she caught a glimpse of the truly sadistic male inside.

She shuddered when she realized that staying with him might be a whole lot worse than wherever she was going. "Is your third party here?" she asked.

"Yep, and I'm about to pass you over and get paid."

"But you don't get paid until the other party confirms I'm the right one he's looking for." He just glared at her. She shrugged and said, "Well, it only makes sense. Nobody wants to do a deal unless they're confirmed on the product."

"Well, they damn well better pay me," he said.

She nodded, didn't say anything for a moment, but then she spoke up again. "Then you have to get Bullard, huh?"

"Oh, I'm sure he'll be along pretty quick. That's what I'm counting on anyway."

"You've got to get paid first," she said.

"Yep, things will be a little bit dicey for a bit, and, if you do anything to screw this up," he said, "you're dead."

And she believed him. He had it all laid out so he could take both prizes without getting caught himself. It was a big gamble on his part, but he obviously had enough confidence to believe he could pull it off. She wondered at men like that. So sure of their ability to get the job done, even in the face of the extreme difficulty he was up against.

Whether it was just confidence or sheer arrogance, she didn't know. She had a lot of confidence in her ability to do her surgical job, but it wasn't arrogance at all. She had worked hard to develop her technical skills, and she knew deep within that her purpose in life was to try her best to save the people who came under her care. But somewhere along the line, she'd lost that confidence to deliver that care.

Or maybe Bullard was right when he'd said she had only lost her way for a while. Did she really want to go back to that? She wanted to go back to helping people, but she didn't necessarily want to go back to an operating room and the pressure she'd been under before. It had been different when her father was alive. She'd still been trying to please him and to follow in his footsteps.

She sighed, not wanting to be too depressed about the whole thing because, right now, she had bigger things on her plate. As soon as she got on deck, her eyes immediately screamed against the sunlight. She cried out, trying to cover up her eyes.

"Yeah, it's bright out here," he said. "Sorry, I don't have a sun hat for you."

Such a snarky tone was in his voice that she realized any pain she suffered would just make him happier. She stiffened and immediately walked over to the edge of the water.

"Go ahead and jump in," he said. "I'll just shoot you." She glared at him, just as he pointed to a boat rapidly coming toward him. "That's your ride."

"Great," she said, "now if only I could figure out how to get away from that bloody doctor."

"Well, I wouldn't worry about the bloody doctor so much," he said. "These guys might decide to keep you themselves, and they'll probably blackmail the doctor to make sure they get an extra payout."

"Would they do that?" she asked in surprise.

"Hell yes," he said. "You're such an innocent."

"I don't live in the world you live in," she said. "Is that so wrong?"

"Nope. If it works, then good for you," he said. "It doesn't work for most people."

"What? Most people aren't dealing with killers like this," she said.

"Lucky them, but some of us were raised in the muck," he snapped, "and it doesn't matter what you say, there's no getting out of it."

"I get that," she said, "but you also had choices in life."

"Save the lesson," he said. "My soul isn't worth saving."

"Glad to hear that," she said. "Then I won't feel guilty when you get taken out in this deal."

"Oh, I won't be taken out," he said, turning to stare at her.

"Well, if you think you'll actually survive this," she said, "you're wrong. These guys will stab you in the back in a heartbeat. And the doctor won't want anybody left alive who knows what's going on."

"Maybe," he said, "but neither do I."

"You could just let me go."

He snorted. "Like that'll happen."

The speedboat coming toward them left a huge white plume of spray behind it. She felt herself shivering inside. A whole new set of men and a whole different set of circumstances. None of it made her feel any better. "You should run," she said suddenly. "I don't feel very good about any of this."

He looked at her and laughed. "Because you don't do these deals, and this is what it's all about," he said. "Don't worry. I'm sure they won't keep you alive for too long."

"Just long enough to hand me over," she said bitterly. "But what makes you think they'll keep you alive?"

"Why wouldn't they?" he said, looking at her.

"You're just lost money to them," she said, with a hard tone. "Didn't you figure that out yet? Anybody who brokers a deal like this doesn't have a problem taking you out at the same time. Why share the profits?"

"That's not how business works," he said, with a sneer. He turned as the boat approached, and he lifted a hand and called out, "Ahoy!"

Then he grabbed her by the arm, dragged her over, and

said, "This is her."

Immediately one man stepped forward. Dark and swarthy, he could have been from any Middle Eastern country, but she'd never seen him before. He looked at her, took several photos, spoke to somebody on the phone, and then nodded. "Good," he said. "Nice job."

Her captor smiled and said, "As long as the pay is good, we're ready," he said. "Where's the money?"

The guy bent down, picked up something from the side, and, sure enough, it was a semiautomatic machine gun. She stared at it in fascination as it started to fire.

She got loose and flung herself to the side, while her captor took multiple bullets, as if dancing midair. By the time the noise stopped, she was curled up in a ball, her hands over her ears, staring in horror at the pulverized body of her kidnapper. And she knew that things had just gone from bad to worse. She was quickly grabbed by the man who had been driving the speedboat and hauled into the new boat, where she was dumped unceremoniously onto the deck. The guy with the gun turned to look at her.

"Don't even talk," he said. "I don't like women to begin with, so, as far as I'm concerned, you're nothing but a piece of baggage that I'll get paid for at the other end. So, shut the fuck up, don't say a word, and I'll keep you alive. I really don't give a shit at this point if the deal goes down or not."

She clamped her mouth tight and nodded.

He turned to the driver and gave him the thumbs-up; then he sat down on one of the big cushioned seats and glared at her. She didn't know what his problem was, but it was obvious he didn't want to be here doing this job. Well, she'd have been perfectly happy if he'd given up on it, but what she didn't want was for him to take his frustration out on her.

Things had already gone from bad to worse, so the last thing she wanted to do was air-dance, like the last guy. She knew it would be a long time before she got the images of his last moments out of her mind. She didn't want to feel sorry for him because he'd asked for everything he'd gotten, but still it was a hard ending to a new life born with so much promise, like all the others, yet some took wrong turns that led to a path of violence and despair. Closing her eyes, she sent out another silent message to Bullard. *Hurry please, damn it. Just hurry!*

"DID YOU JUST see what I saw?" Fallon called back.

"Yeah," Bullard said. "How close are we?"

"Not close enough, and they're running a speedboat."

"Can we disable it somehow?"

"Maybe," Dave immediately signaled Garret to check out the weapons tucked off to the side.

"What do we have here? Because if they get loose on us," Bullard said, "no way in hell we'll catch them."

"We also don't know for sure that they've got her."

At that, Ryland called back from the front of the boat. "Yes, they do. At least if we've got the right female." He handed his phone to Bullard to check the photo.

"That's Leia," he said, excited. "Now we have to track him."

"Or we take him out here," Dave said.

"What are the chances of doing that without getting her killed?" he said.

"Not as good as we'd want them to be."

"They may not be racing away from here anyway,"

Bullard said, and, making a sudden decision, he pointed to the right and said, "Head back toward the mainland."

Ryland looked at him in surprise.

"We can't get close enough to him from here. We don't want to spook him, but we do want to make sure everybody has eyes on him." He turned to Dave and said, "Call Ice and ask for satellite tracking."

"Got it," Dave replied.

Bullard turned to Ryland. "Come on. Let's go. Let's go."

Ryland nodded his head and said, "If you say so."

"I do," he said. "These guys are here for business. They took that guy out in no time, so he was just hired to find and kidnap her, but they didn't want to spend the money to pay him off."

"You know what? This sounds like everyone else we've been dealing with," Ryland said. "That is what happened everywhere we went as we tracked down leads on you or followed up on the attacks on us. They never left anyone behind."

"Well, I don't know if it's connected to us or not," Bullard said, "but enough bad guys are in the world to keep us all hopping."

"That there is," Ryland said, as he pulled on the controls, changing the course enough that anybody looking at them wouldn't have suspected they were heading toward the boat. As they watched, the speedboat turned and headed back in the same direction they were going, and, because Bullard and his crew were closer to the coast, they were likely to end up almost cutting them off. Bullard considered that for a long moment, then decided that he'd probably be better off to find out who was at the other end of this.

As much as he hated to keep her in captivity any longer,

if he could get close enough to see who these men were, at least they could track down who was doing the transaction for her. Maybe it was these guys; Bullard didn't know. What he didn't want was to have her spend the rest of her life looking over her shoulder and wondering when the next attack would come. As it was, as they got closer and closer to the shore, these guys appeared to be following them. "Interesting," Bullard muttered.

"Yeah, not exactly making me feel very good though," Dave replied.

"Do you think they're tracking us?" Bullard asked.

"I wouldn't be at all surprised. If they thought we were out there because of them, they would."

"In which case, everybody needs to be on high alert," Bullard said.

"They've got heavier firepower than we do," Dave said.

"Yeah, but they still have to know how to use it," Bullard replied. "That was incredible overkill before. Like rage or somebody just happy to kill," he said. "I don't think there was anything businesslike about it."

They were still about one hundred yards offshore and moving along the coast, when Ryland signaled from up front.

Bullard made his way up. "What's up?"

"They're gaining on us," he said. "They're following directly in our wake."

"Is that a problem?"

"I'm not sure," Ryland said. "Is there any reason for them to think it's us?"

He fell silent for a moment. "I don't know," he said, "unless she was the bait to bring us out."

At that, Ryland took one look at him, his gaze wide, and

suddenly called out, "Hang on, everybody." He immediately turned the boat, making a hard left to come up even closer against the shore. The boat behind him followed suit. "Shit," he said. "I would highly suspect that's exactly what happened."

"Get Kano on the phone," Bullard called back to Dave.

"Already there," he said, "and Ice is bringing up the satellite on us."

"Good, but it could be too damn late for all of us," Bullard said. Just as they reached the shore, a good twenty feet off, he took one look backward and saw the speedboat behind them.

The gunman stood up with his weapon.

"Jump!" he roared. Just as he hit the water, the air above him split with bullets.

CHAPTER 13

LEIA CRIED OUT in shock and horror as the boat exploded, wood and fiberglass shattering everywhere. Of the men she saw no sign, but how could they possibly have avoided that onslaught of bullets? Tears dripped down her face as she stared at what had once been a boat and several men. She looked at the shooter, who stood there laughing, as proud as he could be.

"You're a monster," she cried out, but immediately he turned the gun on her. She sucked in her breath but refused to let her gaze drop. "How is it you can do something like that and laugh?"

"Because it was fun," he said, with a flick of his wrist. "They were after us, and now we got them. We have to confirm that they can't come after me anymore. Plus, there's a price on Bullard's head to boot. Besides, I'm not against having a second payout for this job."

"So you already knew about both jobs, didn't you?"

"Of course," he said. "Why would I pay somebody when I can take the money myself?" He turned and looked at his driver. "Go to the shore and make sure Bullard is down."

She turned her gaze to the spot where the boat had disappeared. She knew there wasn't a chance that anybody could have survived, but, since Bullard had survived so much worse, she had to wonder. Her stomach sick, she watched anxiously. The pilot pulled up closer, did a couple swoops around at a very slow pace, looking and waiting to see if anybody surfaced. She watched as the gunman walked from side to side, searching.

He fired a couple potshots, then shrugged. "Nobody has surfaced," he said. Then he looked at the driver. "You see anyone?"

"No, I don't. But we don't get paid if we don't get the damn bodies."

"Right," he said. "I didn't think of that." He frowned. "Get a team down here to search." He pulled out his phone and rattled out some orders in a different language.

She sat with her knees tight against her chest, and her arms wrapped around her knees, rocking back and forth. In her mind, she was whispering, *Please no, please no, please make sure nobody was here to take out.* Even as she sat here, she felt a hand on her back. She froze and heard a whisper and twisted slightly. Bullard was there, his hands reaching for her. Before she realized what had happened, he pulled her into the water, like a seal. Once underneath, his lips brushed over the top of hers, as he moved her away from the boat. She knew that the gunman would be there, so she tried to kick hard, but he held her still against him, his legs strong and powerful as he moved deeper and deeper and deeper.

Just when she thought she couldn't breathe anymore, he shifted toward land. When they surfaced, he placed a finger against her lips, rolled her onto her back and held her under, but just enough for her mouth to surface. She opened up her mouth, gasping for air, and, as soon as she caught another breath, she was pulled under once again. She stared at him in shock, and he moved her again, this time toward something that she couldn't really see from underneath. He surfaced beside her; this time her whole head was allowed to come up, and she lay here gasping, trying to catch her breath.

"Are you okay?" he asked hoarsely, holding her close.

She wrapped her arms around his chest, so he wasn't totally supporting her. "I'm okay. Are you?" she asked. "I was terrified when he started firing at you."

"He can keep firing all he wants," Bullard said. "He may have taken out our boat, but we certainly are capable of handling them."

"He's psychotic," she said. "He doesn't give a shit. He killed the kidnapper just so he didn't have to pay him."

"Good," Bullard said in a calm voice. "Saves me that job." She looked at him in surprise, but he just smiled, then leaned over and kissed her gently on her cold lips. "Now we'll get you back safely."

"Well, that would be a dream," she said, "but there's still that damn doctor."

He nodded. "I know. But I don't understand what that's about after all this time." As she hesitated, his gaze narrowed. "Come on. Tell me why he's still after you."

"I have a recording of him talking to somebody," she said. "It's in a safe deposit box in New York. I didn't even listen to all of it. I just realized it would get me killed, and I threw it in there and ran."

"Does he know you have it?"

She shook her head and said, "I can't imagine that he does. Nobody else knew about it. I think he's just trying to make sure, now that I have surfaced, that I won't cause him more trouble."

"That was my take, but, if you have any proof," he said, "we need it."

She gave him a sad smile. "It won't be proof. He'll wiggle away, just like he did last time."

"Maybe not," Fallon said, coming up beside her.

She looked at him and asked, "Are you okay too? Anyone hurt?"

"We're all fine," he said. "We've got people coming to get us."

She nodded slowly. "And somebody who can handle this guy?"

Just then, two speedboats came whipping through the water. At the noise, she looked over.

"Stay down," Bullard snapped, pulling her closer.

"Who are they?" she murmured.

"Ours," Fallon said.

She looked at him in surprise. "So fast?"

"Yeah. We've got more men all around. Don't worry."

"Don't worry, he says," she said, with a broken laugh. "My life was so calm not very long ago," she said, "and now it's turned to chaos again."

"That's not necessarily a problem," Bullard murmured. "It's probably a good thing at this point in time. You need to be moving forward in life."

She groaned. "I blame you for this."

"And I take full responsibility too," he said. "I still think it's better for you."

"I prefer living in my hideaway," she murmured, staring at him.

"I'm sure you do, and I can't say that I wouldn't mind spending a lot of time there myself," he said. "But we still have to deal with the business of living."

"I was dealing just fine," she snapped.

He chuckled and pulled her closer. Yelling came from the side, but he wouldn't let her see what was happening; he remained strong and steady. He looked at her and smiled. "Are you really okay?"

"I am, yes," she muttered against his chest. "But it sucks. I was away from all the violence and human depravity, and now I'm back in it again."

Just then someone called out, "Ahoy!" Gunfire rang out, and she winced and ducked under the water instinctively.

He pulled her back up. "Listen. We may have to dive again," he said, "so stay calm and quiet. Slow down your breathing, if you can."

She clung to him, her body chilled once again, after barely having enough time to warm up between her kidnappers. But Bullard was a fire in and of himself. Just this huge massive stalwart brick of flame. She cuddled up as close as she could.

"It will be okay," he promised.

She squeezed her arms around his neck and just hung on to him. He held her close, and she loved the feeling of being secure in his arms. "Does this mean I'm coming with you then?" she asked, with a burble of nervous laughter.

"It means you're coming with me, wherever I go," he said, "just to keep you safe."

"But that won't be at my island, will it?" she said sadly. "How about we come back to the island for half the year?"

"How about at least a couple times a year for a long visit?"

She pulled back, glaring at him.

He grinned. "Maybe we should use it as a hideaway for all my company."

She thought about that. "I think they'll need a bigger cabin," she muttered.

He chuckled. "Maybe we can buy some other lots there

and build enough for several of us to go there at a time. I have a dozen guys at any given time, and, according to what I've heard from the others, several of them got partners while I was away."

At this point, Dave just chuckled. "You don't know the half of it."

"And that will be a joy to have them all there," she said. Then she looked at Dave and smiled. "Do you have a partner?"

Dave shook his head. "Nope," he said, "but maybe after seeing all these guys and Bullard find someone special, I might just be tempted."

She reached out and said, "You and me both. I had decided I wouldn't ever go back into the world again. Mostly because of that damn asshole doctor."

"Well, you can't let him determine what you do with me," Bullard said.

She turned and looked him straight in the eye. "What about your feelings for Ice?"

He looked at her in surprise, smiling gently. "I will always love Ice," he said calmly. "But my heart is big enough to love more than one woman." She frowned at that, but he reached up and chucked her under the chin. "Ice belongs to another man," he said. "We've never been lovers, and we never will be."

She said, "I'm being foolish, aren't I?"

"No," he said, "you're insecure, and I understand that. Now it's my job to make you feel confident in yourself and in the two of us." Just then, a ton of commotion was heard off to the side. "But first we have to focus on this."

NOW THAT HE had her safely by his side, Bullard wouldn't let her go. He didn't care how her arguments flew from one side to the other. She was staying with him; then he would find this asshole of a doctor. Then he had to deal with his own issues too. He was putting her in danger by hitching her life to his, but together they were stronger. All alone, she was vulnerable, and, as his last flight came to mind, he remembered he wasn't exactly immune from sabotage and assassination attempts either.

He recognized the voices, and, as the boat came around, he felt her trembling in his arms. But, sure enough, Kano was on one boat, driven by Cain. Bullard swam with her over to the side, and, with help, they lifted her into the boat and then him. Fallon and Garret were there as well. As was Dave. With everybody up in the boat, they distributed the weight between the two speedboats, the other one driven by Eton. They all looked at Bullard, their faces wide with grins.

"Damn," Bullard said, "it's good to see you guys all together."

"Ditto," Eton said.

"Quinn is really bummed he's not here," Fallon said, "but he'll be healed up in no time."

At that, the smile fell off Bullard's face. "This asshole, whoever he is, has a lot to answer for."

"I know. I know," Dave said. "And we'll get there. We will. Honest."

Bullard nodded. "We also have to help—" He looked over to Leia, curled up next to him, her arms around her knees, and said, "Everybody, this is Leia. She's the only reason I'm still alive today." All the men looked at her, and, embarrassed at the attention, she lifted a few fingers and gave a small wave.

"Hey, guys," she said. Then her teeth started to chatter. With a muffled exclamation, Dave went to one of the back panels in the boat and pulled out a heating blanket. He quickly wrapped her up.

"Come on, guys," Bullard said, "we've got to get back to base. We've rescued her, but we don't have whoever he was supposed to hand her over to," he said. "The gunman should have something on his person." The men in the second speedboat headed back over to where the gunman's boat drifted.

Leia watched as they transferred to the other boat and searched the bodies. When they had everything they could possibly find, they headed back to their boat, and together, the two speedboats took off, quickly picking up speed.

Wrapped in a solar blanket, she felt some of her strength returning, but shock was setting in as well. Bullard kept an eye on her, but he wasn't at all happy with her color. He sat beside her and picked her up and settled her in his lap.

"I never really realized how big you were," she muttered.

"That's because you're the one who's been looking after me," he said. "Now it's my turn to look after you."

"I've got a better idea," she said. "Why don't we go back to the island and live an idyllic life together in paradise?"

He chuckled. "How much idyllic life do you think we'll get, now that the world knows we're both alive?"

"So what's next?" she asked, with a sigh.

"First, we'll get a hotel and get you warmed up. Then we'll have your purse and ID brought over from the island, then get flights arranged and head to New York."

She groaned. "Do I have to go?"

"Yep, you sure do," he said, "because we'll take down this Leo guy once and for all."

"What about you?" she asked. "I'm just in more danger by being close to you," she said, reiterating his own thoughts from earlier.

"Absolutely," he said. "You are. But, at the same time, that's really not much of an issue just now."

She stared at him in outrage. "How is it not an issue?"

"Just look at how many men I have," he said. "They usually work alone or in pairs, spread out all over the world. To have this many together is like having our own personal army."

She groaned and tucked up close. "Are you sure?"

He realized, in that moment, that she wasn't talking about anything but them. He leaned down and kissed her gently on the nose. Then on the lips and then on each cheek and her forehead, finally coming back to claim her lips in a deep soul-drugging kiss that had her sagging. When he finally lifted his head, he answered her question. "I'm sure."

"I don't want it to be about gratitude," she muttered.

A great big belly laugh rolled from his chest. She was amazed, and he just smiled. "Honey, I don't do things like that out of gratitude."

"Not that, but it's hard to know what else it could be," she said. "You don't even know me."

"I know everything that matters," he said and hugged her even closer. "Stop fighting it. This was ordained."

She snorted. "That would mean everything that happened in the hospital and at my paradise island was ordained too, you know?"

"Sometimes it makes you wonder," he said quietly. "Leia, I'm a different man than I was when that plane blew up. I was very driven back then and didn't really care about looking after myself. I was out to be the champion and to take over the world. I was big and strong, you know?" He paused. "Now I feel very different," he said. "I no longer have to have offices all over the world. I feel much more content at the idea of going home and making a new life for myself there."

She tilted her head back. "But you already had a life there."

"Yes, and it was a male-dominated, action-oriented life, but it lacked what I needed the most, which was a partner and that love to keep me centered and grounded."

"Do you think you have that now?" she challenged.

Neither of them appeared to care about anybody else listening in, and, as Bullard looked around, he saw that the guys were trying to give them some privacy. They were all just damn happy that he'd moved on from Ice, which had just been an ongoing heartbreak for Bullard and his team.

Bullard had never moved on from Ice but he'd also never even sought out a partner, thinking none could ever equal what he felt for Ice. But he had found someone. Without even looking, he had. He looked down at her. "Absolutely."

CHAPTER 14

I T SEEMED LIKE several hours, but it was probably less than two before Leia stood under a hot shower in a hotel room. Bullard was talking with his team in the common room linking several connected suites. They were all working on a plan for the next stage. She had no clue what the next stage was and was still desperately trying to get warm. She needed food, and she needed rest. The food they could probably get but the rest? She wasn't so sure.

Everybody was wired now that they all had reconnected and were together, simply enjoying the fact that Bullard was alive. She had experienced the pain of dealing with the loss of having Bullard to herself, if only for a short time, and she saw that the months of loss and uncertainty had taken a toll, and the others just couldn't seem to calm down. She got right away that they were a huge family; something she'd never had.

When she finally turned off the water, she wrapped herself up in a towel and sat on the edge of the bathtub. It just felt so strange to be here; yet, at the same time, it also felt right. Her island was where she wanted to be, and, while she could understand Bullard's need to return to his life, she wondered if she could live wherever he needed her to. They were on their way to New York, and then they would fly back home to wherever his base was. In Africa, which she couldn't even imagine.

But, according to the others, she would really like it. Particularly the surgery suite. She frowned at that, wondering if medicine was something she should even be working in anymore. Her skills were rusty. She sat here, looking down at her hands, wondering about that. Five years was a long time. And just like she had adjusted to being back at a hotel, she wondered if being back in an OR would feel exactly the same, as if she'd just had a short holiday away. When a knock came on the bathroom door, she called out a response, "Yes?"

"Are you okay?" Bullard asked, as he turned the knob and stepped in, without waiting for an invitation. She looked up at him, smiled, and said, "I'm fine. Outside of the fact that I have nothing to wear, that is."

He nodded and held out her dress, which he had apparently managed to dry. But then it didn't take much. It was the loose and flimsy island wear she had become so accustomed to. By the time they got it to her, it was 90 percent dry anyway. She looked at it and nodded, realized she had likely fared better in that department than the men. "That'll be something, thank you."

"I can send somebody back to the island to get the rest of your personal effects too," he said, "if you need them right away. Otherwise we'll ship them out."

"I don't need them right away," she said, "but I will want them eventually."

"Good," he said. "We have flights booked for the States tomorrow morning."

"Great," she said, almost sadly. "You know that no part of me wants to go to New York."

"If I thought we had any other way to deal with Leo, I

wouldn't ask you to," he said. "It's not like I want to put you through that."

"Why would he even be in New York, when I was in the South Pacific?"

"Because we have confirmed a booked flight for him, returning to New York. If I thought we could stop it and face him in Australia or something, I would," he said. "But he's booked on a direct flight to New York, and it left about forty minutes ago."

"Do we know for sure that he is on it?"

"In terms of electronic check-in data, yes," he said.

She groaned. "So how did he find out so fast?"

"We figured that the third-party guy picking you up was giving him updates, and they probably had a rendezvous point, but, when everything blew up and when they didn't show up with you, Leo ran."

"It still seems too fast."

"Well, maybe he planned to bring you back to New York. Or maybe instead of meeting you in person," he said, "he would meet you over a video. Or maybe all he wanted was a video of your death," he said. "I don't know."

"Anything is possible," she said. "We need to get everything out of my safe deposit box anyway," she said, "and I can arrange for a few other things while I'm in New York."

"Is there anybody you want to visit?"

"No way," she said. Then she groaned and said, "No, it's all over with."

"Actually it isn't. Apparently a few doctors have been pushing for an investigation. There's a lot of hard feelings over what happened and how you were treated."

"It's been five years," she said. "Why would they care now?"

"Because other people have died," he said gently.

She stared at him, shocked at first, then nodded. "Of course. It's not like this asshole has changed his colors."

"Exactly. While we're there, do you want to speak with anybody on the board?"

"Nope, I sure don't," she said. "They had their chance five years ago." He studied her for a long moment, and she glared at him. "Why would I go back and face all that nonsense, when I can just go to the bank, pick up what I want, and leave. I don't even have an apartment there."

"Well, I think a detective would like to talk to you."

"A detective?" She stopped and stared. "Why would a detective want to talk to me now?"

"Because the other doctors have brought in law enforcement."

She snorted. "And they'll just want me to go through all that bullshit again," she said. "It was a cover-up, and nobody gave a shit. If they've got new murders, they can deal with those."

"And I get that," he said. "Really I do. I also get that this isn't what you want to do, but we're trying to make sure this Leo guy can't go kill anybody else."

"Well, I would be happy if the entire board lost their jobs," she said stiffly. "Not to mention a few of the other doctors, who seemed more than happy to throw me to the wolves."

"Give me their names," he said coolly, "and I'll make sure it happens."

She stared at him in shock. "You can't do that," she said.

He smiled. "Honey, if you want heads to roll, I can make sure they roll," he said. "You want jobs to be lost? I'll make sure they're lost."

"Can you do that?" She didn't even know how she felt about somebody having that kind of power.

"I can," he said calmly. "The fact that you are justified in how you feel and that they let a murderer run loose to kill more people is absolutely something they need to pay for."

"They won't do anything," she said. "They'll brush it all under the rug."

"And maybe not," he said. "For you, sweetie, I would do anything." And, with that, he turned and walked back out, calling out to her behind him, "We've ordered food and coffee. It should be here in about ten minutes."

With that, she slowly stood and got dressed. She took a moment to brush her wet hair and put it into a long braid. Her sun-bleached blond hair had been looking a little worse for wear, but, after the shower and a shampoo, it had returned to its former silky state. But she didn't want to leave it flying around. So, with it plaited down her back, she rehung her towels and the robe, and stepped out, suddenly aware of the onslaught of men. As one, they all turned to look at her. She frowned. "So," she said a little stiffly. "Do I pass inspection?"

Bullard snorted. "Don't mind them," he said, as he walked over and wrapped an arm around her shoulders. Facing them, he said, "They all know what'll happen if they give you any trouble."

The men all snorted and chuckled among themselves. "We don't have anything but our thanks to give her," Fallon said. He walked over, introduced himself, and said, "It's nice to meet you, Leia. Thank you for saving Bullard." Then one by one, every single one of the men followed in line and did something similar.

By the time they were done, tears were threatening to

spill onto her cheeks. "You do know it was just luck that I found him, right?"

The men grinned, made teasing comments about their boss.

"Seriously, I was out one day and saw him floating, caught up in the weeds. He was just too damn big and ornery to leave there. He lifted his head and looked at me. Then he passed out, and I knew I had to help him."

"And you stayed hidden all that time? Was it partly because of the damn doctor?" Fallon asked.

She took a long slow breath and shook her head. "No, I thought I had dealt with all that years ago by moving out of the country and living in my sanctuary. But I felt strongly that Bullard was in danger," she said, "and I had no idea who or how to contact anyone, so I did hang on to the news of finding him for a long time, waiting for his memories to return. Keep in mind, he was in very, very bad shape, and it would have been very risky to move him at that point anyway."

With a sideways glance at Bullard, she went on. "But once he started getting up and moving around outside, the islanders asked me more and more questions, and I knew the news would get out. By the time Bullard remembered enough to tell me who the good guys were, and we got a cell phone, his news was well and truly around the globe already." She grinned up at him. "You sure look different now, compared to the way you did when I dragged you onto my skiff and in the weeks following."

"I can't even imagine how you managed to get me on there," he said, "or into that little hut."

"Well, the hut was my yoga platform originally although I had to expand and modify it for you," she said. He stared at her in shock, as she shrugged. "The floor was already there. It was a little bit of a dock, so first I built a bed and filled it with lots of straw and fronds, then I managed to drag you up onto that, one foot at a time, and that's where you stayed. I put the supports around the sides to keep you from falling out, and the netting around it afterward." He stared at her in shock. She said, "What the hell was I supposed to do? I weigh 118 pounds, and what are you, two-fifty?"

"Two-fifty now," he said, with a nod. "An easy three hundred before."

She nodded. "So, no way in hell I could get you up to my hut. But that platform was already there, so I just turned it into your own little space. Then, of course, came the surgery." Her voice dropped at that.

"That all just makes a lot of sense on so many levels," Bullard said, studying her contemplatively. "You have my gratitude for keeping me alive, and now this team will do our best to keep you alive."

"I didn't think my life was in any danger," she murmured. "But now I'm not so sure."

"Well, we know quite differently now," he said. "Your life is absolutely in danger. We just don't know how much effort the doctor will put forth to take it."

"And I just don't understand why," she said. "Even if there's already an investigation, maybe it would make sense if I were a key witness or something, but obviously I'm not."

The men looked at each other, and one of them cleared his throat and said, "You actually could be."

"No," she said, "I won't be. They put me through hell back then, and I have no intention of going back into that zoo."

"Maybe not, but you could be called as a witness regardless."

She frowned at him. "In that case, I'm going back to my island."

"What we won't do," Bullard said, "is panic. We'll talk to the detectives and see what it is they need from you."

She glared at him. "Or not."

He rolled his eyes. "It's nuts we're even having this conversation."

"Of course it is," she said. "I was there. You weren't." And, with that, she walked over to the small chair by the window and sat down. "Now that we've discussed that as far as I'll go," she said, "didn't you say food was coming? I'm starving."

Right on cue, a knock came at the door. One of the men went to answer it, and several large trolleys were pushed inside.

As soon as the door closed, she walked over and lifted the domes. "You really meant it when you said food, didn't you?"

"I told you that I'd look after you," Bullard said.

"Not your job," she replied. "I'm perfectly capable of looking after myself." She shot him a thunderous look. "I get that you want to do something for me, and, if there's nothing else, then let me go back to my island."

"Not until you're safe," he said. "You have admit that it's just not a safe place for you right now."

She stared out the window and nodded. "That may very well be," she said, "but I won't give up my island property. It's the place that healed my soul."

"You won't have to," he said. "I would never ask you to do that. Now let's drop the heavy discussion and eat."

But she was afraid that dropping the discussion was just

pushing it off to another point in time when he figured she'd be more amiable. She just didn't understand how seeing the detective or dealing with this issue would help in any way. She stopped and looked at him. "What if we don't leave here and just talk to him over the phone?"

"It still doesn't get your thumb drive back."

She frowned. "Maybe I don't want it back."

"Maybe so, but, if anything's on there to nail the doc with, then we need to get it."

She frowned.

He shook his head and said, "Come on. Just eat for now."

She glared, then opened her mouth to the forkful he popped in. She had to admit that, by the time she finished eating, she felt a little bit better, although the steady stream of lighthearted banter among the team undoubtedly helped. The men were clearly still feeling giddy with relief and celebrating Bullard's survival. While they officially hadn't given up hope, she saw in their gazes that they had each been mourning his loss, perhaps Dave most of all.

As for her, she was still scared and completely reluctant to go back to New York, but she wanted to take care of a few things at some point in time. So she decided that a quick trip would be okay. She realized that, on some level, she was afraid that, if she went to New York, she'd never get back out again, and that was the underlying cause of her stress over the topic. She was fearful that, when she got back into the nastiness, she might end up jailed on murder charges, which is what she had been threatened with in the first place.

Did she want the doctor charged? Yes, of course, but only if they kept her out of it. Because, as she had come to realize, a bit of a coward was in her right now, and she didn't want to even deal with Leo. But, if he was the one who had put a price on her head and was even now still looking for her, then it had to be resolved. Otherwise she would never be safe, and that would ruin her life.

He'd already done that once, so she didn't want to give him the power to do it again.

BY THE TIME the arrangements were finalized, everybody headed to New York by air. She stuck fairly close to Bullard's side all the way to the airplane, and he understood. He didn't want to take her back into this trauma that had eclipsed her world before, any more than she wanted to go. She'd been a gifted surgeon, widely recognized as an upcoming star with the power to conquer the world. Instead somebody had destroyed that bright star and had blasted her life to oblivion, sending her underground to attempt to rebuild a sense of safety on her own.

Bullard understood how that would feel because he'd had such a similar reaction himself. But her story couldn't be allowed to stop there. She couldn't be allowed to walk away from her gift and everything that had mattered to her because of a fear of it happening all over again. He desperately wanted her to come to Africa and to live with him there, but he also wasn't prepared to force her to do that.

She'd been kidnapped and smuggled away, had witnessed a violent murder, then essentially had been kidnapped again. Her life in imminent danger the whole time. The last thing he wanted to do was treat her in a way that would bring up those memories at the hand of yet another asshole. He looked at her, but she still had her eyes closed as she leaned against the window. He hoped she was sleeping, but it was hard to tell.

The other guys periodically turned and looked at him, as if checking to see if he were really here, and he just smiled and nodded. They'd split up the team and were taking two different routes, just to make sure they didn't all die in one big accident. Not that he believed in accidents anymore, since it was obvious that the entire team had been targeted.

They still hadn't gotten any further in figuring out who was behind it all, but right now it was all about Leia, and he wasn't sure when they could turn their attention to resolving the issue of who was trying to take down his whole operation. His mind kept churning, as they searched for more information. He had emails and text messages from both Levi and Ice, but, so far, nobody was having any luck tracking down who this person was. It had to be somebody close to him, and that was the part that really bothered him.

Somebody who had access to the compound.

After finishing their business in New York, they would head back to Africa, and he couldn't wait for that to happen. He'd already sent Dave and two men back there, while Bullard was heading to New York with the others. Just because there were still so many questions at this point, he wanted to keep the teams equally balanced. He thought about sending a couple more back, but, so far, everybody was more or less on board with splitting the team up as he had. He had a couple other guys off on missions he would bring back to his main base compound, and he also had two men at the African border compound in Tunisia.

He wondered if he even needed to keep that location anymore. What he wanted to do was reevaluate the size and the scope of the work that he was doing. No doubt the world needed what he did, and that business he could continue to grow and grow. He would probably never eclipse the need because the world was such a messed-up place, but maybe he didn't need to be the one who did it. Maybe he should set up some of the men with their own company and have them take on the bigger and more complex jobs in the field, instead of Bullard handling it all.

And whatever he would handle, he wanted to stay closer to home, so he was closer to Leia. This was something he had never really expected to happen, but, as his life was changing, he saw that the need to change was also within him. These last few months had changed how he viewed the world and his role within it. He still didn't exactly know how it would end up, but definitely change was in the air.

She murmured, "What are you thinking about?"

"About change," he said, "and I'm making the arrangements for flights to get us home after this too."

"How long will we stay in New York?"

"I was thinking about thirty-six hours."

Her eyes flew open at that. "Good," she said in a hard voice. "That's about all I can tolerate. I won't sleep for thinking a murder charge will be slapped on my head."

"Not happening," he said. "Hence the timing."

She reached over and squeezed his fingers.

He laced his fingers into hers and smiled. "You'll be okay. I promise."

"All of us, I hope," she said, then settled back to rest.

When they landed, he took charge and quickly whisked them off to a five-star hotel downtown. As she walked through the lobby, always two men were at her side, and she was quickly escorted directly to an elevator instead of registration. She looked at Bullard and Fallon. "Is this how you guys always operate?"

"If we can, yes," Fallon said. "It's best to avoid as many people as we can."

"If you say so."

Up in their rooms, she immediately looked at the huge double bed to one side. She walked over to it, then laid down and said, "I don't know about you guys, but I need to crash."

"Good enough, we'll work in the other room," Bullard said, and he and Fallon moved to the connected suite, leaving the adjoining door open. She wasn't sure how it all worked, but what she started to see was the money needed to do all this and the access Bullard had to a seemingly unlimited amount of resources at a level she hadn't expected. It had never occurred to her that he had that much money, but, to make all this happen, Bullard had to be very wealthy. She wasn't sure how she felt about that. She had money too, but not at his level.

Money had never mattered to her, but it certainly mattered because of what it could do, and obviously he was a pro at making it work for him. Still, it was a surprise to consider that he was that wealthy. Maybe it was his company rather than Bullard personally, but she had no way of knowing. She was too damn tired to even worry about it, and she let her eyes close as she drifted off to sleep. When she woke up later, Bullard lay beside her. She rolled over and looked up at him. "Did you sleep?

He yawned and said, "I caught a few minutes, yeah."

"Do you want to try to sleep longer?"

"Nope," he said, "we have a meeting in two hours. We've got food and coffee coming."

"The coffee's always welcome," she said, with a smile. She got up and looked down at her single dress and said, "Clothes would be nice too."

"We can go out shopping first, if you want," he said.

She shrugged. "I guess it's not that important right now, but my clothing from the island may not be suitable for Africa."

"It probably is actually," he said. "We have a wonderful 74 degrees all year-round."

She looked at him and frowned. "Seriously?"

"Yep," he said, "it's pool season every day."

"Well, maybe my clothes will be okay then," she said. "Did anybody go to my island and check?"

"Yep. All your personal belongings have been packed and shipped out. We already brought you your ID and purse."

"Oh, I hadn't even thought that far ahead. That still doesn't mean I'm not going back, you know?" she said.

"I know," he said. "I'm not trying to take you away from there."

"Liar," she said affectionately.

He burst out laughing. "Okay, so I am for a little bit, but I promise I'll get you back there again."

"Uh-huh," she said, with a nod.

"Did you ever wonder how the world found out about me being there?"

"No," she said. "I've been trying not to think about that too much. Obviously it must have been one of the islanders, but I don't know who."

"The old medicine woman is who I would say."

"Why would you think that?" she asked.

"Because she's the one who seemed to know so much."

"You mean, the thing about Terk?"

"Yeah, and I do know who Terk is now, by the way."

"Good," she said. "I don't understand how the messaging was coming back and forth though."

"Neither do I, but, once I figured out you were getting those kind of messages, I knew where we were at."

"Good for you," she said, "because I sure as hell didn't."

He chuckled. "It's all good."

She shook her head. "And that's just to make me feel better."

A knock on the door interrupted his reply. He looked at his watch and said, "That will be breakfast."

She hopped up and headed into the bathroom, and, by the time she came out, Fallon was there with food on a plate, motioning for her to go serve herself.

"We don't have too much time, do we?" she asked.

"Not too much," he said, "but plenty of time to eat."

CHAPTER 15

AS IT TURNED out, Leia barely had enough time to eat, before Bullard motioned at her that it was time to go. He handed her a big briefcase, and she looked at it and frowned.

"I just found it in the gift shop," he said. "Your ID documents are inside. And I thought you might want this," he said, as he handed her a phone.

"Wow," she said. "You just picked this up too?"

"Yes," he said, "one of my team just delivered new phones, since we took ours swimming. I figured maybe you would want one."

"Maybe," she said, as she studied it with interest. "They've really changed in the last few years."

"They have," he said, "but they're not so different. Easier and faster than the older ones, that's for sure." With that, they headed out toward the elevators. As she turned around inside, and the doors were closing, she saw Fallon still at the hotel room door just down the hall, doing something to the lock. "Don't we want to wait for him?"

"No," he said, "he'll take the stairs, and he'll meet us later."

"So he's following along to make sure we're safe, is that it?" she asked drily.

"Absolutely," Bullard said, with a smile.

When they got outside, she realized that they only had a couple blocks to go to the police station. "Can we just walk?" she asked.

"Yes," he said, "it's probably better anyway. Trying to get a cab would be brutal."

Once they got to the police station, they didn't even have to wait. They were shown right into a room, where the detective introduced himself as Detective Bruce Wilson, then led them to a smaller room.

She looked around in surprise. "This feels like an interrogation room," she said.

"It is," he said, "but we're not here to interrogate you. We are only interested in Dr. Leo Manfred."

"That's funny. Nobody gave a damn five years ago," she said flatly.

He winced at that and said, "Did you actually report him yourself?"

"Yes! I reported everything directly to a detective. Orion Houtser is his name," she said.

Detective Wilson looked up quickly and stared at her. "Five years ago?"

She nodded. "Yes. Why? What did he say? I knew he didn't really believe me, and I never heard back from him," she said. "When the medical board and the hospital told me to disappear or get charged with first-degree murder, it was clear to me that they weren't too interested in listening either," she said.

"Can you please tell me what happened five years ago?" the detective said. "Just leave the other detective out of it for now and tell me what happened."

She closed her eyes, took a deep breath, and quickly went over a shortened version of what she knew. He asked a bunch of questions, and, the whole time, Bullard sat here quietly at her side. She appreciated that.

Detective Wilson sat back when Leia had finished. "I don't suppose you have any proof, do you?" he asked. She looked at him and then down at the floor. He leaned forward. "Do you?" His voice was hard.

"What I have," she said, "is a flash drive with a copy of a recorded conversation. I was transcribing a bunch of my medical notes in a small room, and it's easier with head-phones, so when the doctor entered the outer office and was talking on the phone, he didn't realize I was nearby. In that phone conversation, he said several things. They were alarming, so I recorded it. Don't quote me on the exact wording. It's been a long time," she said. "I'll just repeat some statements that were made, not necessarily in this order or in these exact words."

Closing her eyes, she paused a moment, like she was re-membering. "Okay, Detective, here goes. He said things like, 'Make sure that bitch is dead. I don't want her just gone from the hospital, I want her gone-gone. I would kill her myself if I had the opportunity, but it would look a little too suspicious after her accusations against me. If you want to keep the money flowing, you'll make sure this happens. I don't care how far she disappears or where she goes, I want her found. It's not enough to just ruin her career and get her out of the hospital. She saw me kill him, so what am I supposed to do with that? What if she comes back later and decides that I have to pay for it? ... Hell yes, you'll pay for it too. You're the one who arranges these deals. If you want the money to keep flowing, you'll take care of her. And you can tell Claire and Dawn on the board that they need to stop the squawking about their internal investigation. Otherwise I'm likely to come after them too. ... Of course they don't know. I'm their golden boy, and no way in hell I'll allow Leia to ruin that. We've got a good deal going here. Nobody ever suspects the surgeon, and we're allowed a certain percentage of deaths anyway. I always try to keep my numbers right in the allowable percentage. ... It depends on who's paying the bigger money. I can always get somebody else to make a mistake.' Okay, that's it," she said, sitting back and opening her eyes.

She looked at the detective. "I'm sure there was more, but that's the gist of what's on the recording."

Detective Wilson stared at her in shock. "I don't understand. Why didn't you give it to anybody?"

"I did," she exclaimed, jumping to her feet. "I gave it to that detective," she said. "So you guys knew the whole time."

He stared at her, his hand over his mouth for a moment. Then he looked at Bullard, again at her. "I've never heard or read anything about this tape. And that detective? He's dead."

"What?" she said, instantly going pale, sitting down again.

"Yes. Detective Houtser was in an accident not long after all that blew up. As in it happened at the same time."

Bullard looked at Leia, then said, "What are the chances that he went and talked to your little doctor, who arranged for him to have an accident?"

"Considering the circumstances, I would say it's *very* possible," she said, with a decisive nod. "You don't understand. Leo just kills and doesn't give a shit. It's like it's good fun to do it right under everybody's nose, and he's getting paid for it too."

"Sounds like it," Bullard said. "That very interesting."

"Agreed," said Detective Wilson. "But, at the same time, a very strange scenario. I'm gonna need that file."

"I get it," she said, "but, in order for you to get a copy," she said, "I want some guarantees."

The detective slowly stiffened and glared at her. "I'm not in a—"

"I want to be formally and publicly cleared of all suspicion, and my reputation restored," she said.

He nodded slowly. "I'm good with that."

"I want that doctor brought down," she snapped. "He's also the one responsible for having me kidnapped, but nobody even gives a shit about that," she said. "I want the people on the hospital board at that time replaced. They're the ones who threw me under the bus, even though I didn't do anything."

The detective frowned at that and started to speak, but she interrupted. "And Patricia Marie," she said, "she was a very good doctor, and she also got canned at the same time because she stood up for me. I want her reinstated."

At that, Detective Wilson shook his head. "I don't know that I can make all that happen," he said. "Some of that is well out of my sphere of influence."

She didn't miss a beat and said, "And I don't know if I remember how to get into the safe deposit box."

Bullard gave a hard snort at that and said, "What he can't do, I will."

She looked at him, then gave a clipped nod. "Fine."

The detective looked back and forth between them, settling on Bullard. "You have to stay within the law."

Bullard smiled and said, "Of course."

Wilson glared at him. "I mean it. No taking the law into your own hands."

"Wouldn't dream of it," he said. "I have a lot more sophisticated ways to deal with this mess."

The detective looked at her and asked, "Where is it?"

She looked at Bullard and said, "We need to make a trip to the bank."

"We wanted to go there anyway," he said, standing up.

"Yes," she said and looked at the detective. "You should probably come with us now."

He nodded and stood.

As soon as they were outside the police station, Bullard hailed a nearby cab, which seemed like a miracle, considering it was New York. Once in the back seat, she gave the driver the address of the bank, and they were there within ten minutes. Bullard paid for the cab, and they walked inside. It took another ten minutes to verify her identity, but finally she was led into a small room where she was given her box. Thankfully she had specifically requested a combination lock, rather than a key. With a look at it, she took a deep breath, entered the combination, and opened it.

Bullard whistled at her side. "Wow, I gather you don't trust banks."

"It was emergency money, in case I had to run deeper than I expected," she said, pulling out several stacks of cash. There on the bottom, under the money, was the flash drive. She pulled it out, looked at Bullard, and said, "I'll need to make a copy of this."

Nodding, Bullard opened his hand, where he had a device with a USB port already attached to a cell phone. Holding out his other hand, she gave him the flash drive, which he immediately plugged in and copied the file onto the phone, which he sent off to cloud storage. Once he disconnected it, he handed the drive back to her. "That way you can give the detective the original," he said.

"And the copy you have works?"

He checked it, and they heard the doctor's voice immediately, saying that she was supposed to die, even using her name. Bullard's face was grim.

She just shrugged, clearly disturbed by the sound of the man's voice. "That asshole ruined my life," she said. "I really don't want him to get off too easy. Fifty years in prison sounds about right."

Bullard chuckled and led her out to the waiting room, where the detective waited for her. She handed over the flash drive. The detective looked at it, frowned, and said, "Are you sure it's on here?"

Bullard said, "I have a copy right here." A moment later the recording played.

His face grim, the detective said, "We can get him with this," then looked at Leia. "Anything else?"

"Not that I can think of right now," she said, suddenly feeling really tired.

"Okay," he said. "Now I just need to locate him."

"He flew into New York this morning," Bullard said.

At that, the detective looked at him in surprise. "He did?"

"Yes, and he lives in Chelsea," she said. "At least he did before."

"He still does."

"So I can leave, right?" she asked, her briefcase now heavy with the extra cash. She didn't know that she wanted to leave it here at this bank either. She had a different account that she could access with her cards, and, not knowing where she would end up, she decided just taking the cash was best. She wouldn't need the safe deposit box anymore.

"No. Actually I'd like you to stay at least twenty-four hours."

But Bullard said, "You can have her here until our flight leaves tomorrow morning," he said. "Other than that, we're gone."

The three of them walked outside, and she smiled at Bullard. "Can we leave now, or at least go shopping, maybe get a couple outfits?"

"Sure." Bullard moved her along the sidewalk with purpose.

Just then, a shot rang out.

Bullard already moved Leia into an alcove, as the wall where he'd been standing was hit with a bullet that had swung past his head. The detective was down, taking refuge behind a vehicle and stared at them.

"What do you want to bet that's your doctor?" Bullard said, looking at the detective, who was already swearing. He had his phone out, calling for backup. Bullard glanced at the bank, then at her, and asked, "Does he know about this recording?"

"Maybe the first detective told Leo about the evidence. Maybe that's why that detective is dead. Otherwise, who else would say anything?" she said. Bullard tilted his head. "We could have been followed, I guess," she added. "Or maybe somebody in the bank saw me hand it over." Sirens filled the air soon afterward, but Bullard wouldn't let her move yet. She looked at him and said, "Leo's still trying to kill me, isn't he?"

"He's trying to kill anybody associated with this mess," he said, "and then he'll try to run."

"We'll lock down the airports," the detective said. "We

have to make sure we get him this time."

"You think?" she said, shaking her head. "Nobody gave a shit before."

"Doesn't matter," Bullard said. "We're leaving, and we're leaving now." He looked at the detective. "Are you okay here?"

"Yes," he said, "but don't leave now. That shooter's out there, just waiting for us to make a move."

"My men are here now," Bullard said, and just then a big Hummer rolled up and parked in the middle of the street. He quickly hustled Leia into the back seat. She dove into the back, panicked at the idea that the shooter was still out there.

Fallon was driving. "Are you guys okay?"

"We are. Where is the rest of the team?"

"They're looking for the shooter," he said. "I'm getting you back to the hotel."

"Do you think Leo did it himself?" she asked.

"No," Bullard said. "He's hired somebody else to do all his dirty work so far. He likes to kill on one level in a medical setting, but this is more like taking out the garbage to him."

"How about we take out his garbage?" she snapped.

"I'm all for it," Bullard said. "We've just got to catch the bastard."

She looked at Fallon. "Thanks for the pickup."

He grinned. "Not a problem."

"You didn't see him when you were out there, did you?" Bullard asked Fallon.

"Actually I think I did," he said, then held up his phone. "Is this him?"

She looked at a picture of her nemesis and felt almost

faint. "That's him," she whispered.

"Yeah, he was at the hotel."

She stared at him. "How would he know we were there?"

"It wouldn't be hard," Bullard said. "We pretty well put out a bulletin that you were coming back."

"Jesus!" She stared at him. "Did you use me as bait?"

"We used all of us as bait," he said. "What we had to do was make sure he showed his hand."

"Well, he did," she snapped, "but he could have killed somebody out there."

"Well, let's hope he comes a little closer to try again," he said, his voice hard.

She sank back into the soft upholstery of the back seat. "Where are we going now?"

"We'll return to the hotel," he said. "You want to catch this guy, right?"

"Yes, you're damn right, I do," she snapped. "I suppose you were making all these plans while I was sleeping."

"Yep," he said, "some of them anyway. A lot of it depended on what kind of tricks this guy would pull."

"How do we know that the shooter didn't get away and isn't coming after us now?"

Just then Fallon's phone went off, and he tossed it to Bullard, who answered it to hear Kano's voice. "Kano, what's up?" Bullard said, putting it on Speakerphone.

"Shooter's dead," he said.

"Oh, I'm so sorry to hear that," Bullard said, but he had a big fat grin in his face.

Leia stared at him in shock. "You enjoy this, don't you?"

"I love bringing down assholes," he said. "I told you that he won't bother you again."

BULLARD MEANT IT too. He'd watched her completely not care about the money in her safe deposit box, other than the fact that it could buy her safety. He understood that. The fact that she wouldn't ever have to worry about funds again wasn't something that had registered yet. He had money galore. The thing about money was what you could do with it. And everybody else just seemed to hold it. He smiled as he listened to Kano give him the details.

"Call the detective," Bullard said and gave him the name and number of the guy they had just left. "He'll want to hear from you," he said. "We're heading back to the hotel."

"Good enough," Kano said. "Watch yourselves."

"Oh, we're watching," he said. "This guy may have run out of people hired to do the job, which should push him into trying himself, and he doesn't have the skills of his paid assassins."

At that, she interrupted him, leaning forward and saying, "Of course he does. It's just that his weapon of choice is a scalpel."

"Right," Bullard said, as he hung up the phone. As soon as Fallon pulled up in front of the hotel, Bullard hopped out and reached to help her down and said, "We're going straight upstairs."

"Fine," she said, brushing ahead of him. "But when this is over, you owe me a holiday." He laughed with great joy, tucked her hand into his elbow, and asked, "Where would you like to go?"

"I think Africa," she said. "And if you don't have a place as nice as mine, we're going back to the island."

"Hey, anything you want to change, you can change," he said, "but, before you make any decisions, give it a chance to work its way into your heart."

"Is it that good?"

"Definitely," he said. "I have some photos I can show you when we get upstairs."

She sighed. "You know what? Really, if you'll be there ..."

"Ditto, sweetie," he said, with a smile.

She groaned. "That doesn't mean I'll be a surgeon again."

"Nope. It sure doesn't," he said. "I handle most of the surgeries myself anyway."

"Ah," she said, "so you don't want the competition."

He burst out laughing at that. "I don't know if you'll allow the competition," he said. "My training was a lot rougher than yours, but I've been helping people in my community for a long time. Medical care is too expensive and too far away for most people."

"You do surgery for free?"

"For free? Hell no. For chicken or for squash. It depends on what they can pay."

She burst out laughing at that, and then she saw he was serious. "You mean it, don't you?"

"I do," he said. "I've often thought about expanding it a lot more but haven't really had the time or the opportunity, but I run clinics on a regular basis."

"Interesting," she murmured.

"I've been trying to get Dave's niece, Lindsey, to come on board too," he said. "Apparently some think maybe she will, now that she and Fallon are an item."

"Then you don't need me," she said. "Isn't she a surgeon?"

"Yeah, but I'm not exactly sure what specialty she ended up going into," he admitted. "Besides, the last few months have changed a few things for a lot of us."

By now they were in the elevator, heading up to their set of rooms. As they walked down the hallway, he checked the door, then unlocked it and let her in.

"What were you checking for?" she asked curiously, as she stepped into the room.

"To see if anybody disturbed it."

"Well, housekeeping should have been in by now, shouldn't they?"

"No, I haven't let them service the rooms yet," he said, "but the door wasn't disturbed anyway."

"But there are connecting doors," she said, with a laugh. "How can you be sure he didn't go in that side?"

He looked at her and walked toward the connecting door between the two rooms and checked. "Well, nobody's come through yet," he said, but, with that, he put a hard lock on it.

She frowned. "You really think he's coming?"

"I really hope so," he said, with a fat smile.

She rubbed her eyes and said, "Do you think we could order up some tea?"

"Sure," he said. "Do you want something else with it?"

She thought about it, shrugged, and said, "I don't know, maybe a sweet of some sort."

"Good enough," he said. "Let's have a look at the room service menu, and we'll get it ordered," he said, "or I could send someone out for something different."

"Oh, gosh no, that's way too much trouble. I'm not nearly that high maintenance."

He chuckled at that, remembering the simple fare on her island. "What do you want to do with all that money in your briefcase?"

"Well, I need to do something with it," she said. "It's a pretty large amount to be packing around."

"You didn't want to leave it in that bank, I take it?"

"No, that's not my normal bank," she said, "so I didn't want to have to open a separate account that I would rarely use."

"So what bank do you want to go to?"

She named the one that she used all the time. He quickly searched for the closest location and said, "One is not too far from here, so we can handle that in a little bit."

"Good," she said, and she sank down on the couch. "Will Fallon be okay out there?"

"Yep, they'll all be okay," he said. "Let me check in with Dave back at the base." As she listened, he called Dave back home. It was a quick discussion, just to exchange updates and ascertain that everything was okay.

She said, "Sounds like you run a tight ship."

"Always have," he said, with a laugh. "But you never quite know when things can go south on you."

"Isn't that the truth," she said sadly.

"Well, hopefully something will let us get out of here soon enough." He looked at her, smiled, and said, "We're leaving in the morning, not to worry."

"Says you," she said, "unless they stop us."

"They'll have to do more than just stop us," he said.

She didn't say anything else. The room service cart arrived not long afterward, and, when the server knocked on the door, Bullard got up, checked through the peephole, and asked for ID. Bullard tipped the delivery person and took the trolley from him, closing and locking the door, before pushing it through the suite. He neared her and said, "The tea is here."

"Good," she said, staring at him. "We are safe, aren't we?"

"For the moment, yes," he said. And, with that, she had to be satisfied. "Anybody else you want to tell that you're in town?"

She thought about it, then shook her head. "No," she said, "I said my goodbyes back then."

"So, you're ready for a new start."

"Maybe," she said. "I still feel like I have to say goodbye to the island."

"I'm serious," he said, "we can go back there on a regular basis. You don't have to say goodbye."

"I would like that very much," she said quietly.

"I would too," he said. "It's a very special place, and I don't want to lose it myself. I have a lot of good memories there."

"Huh," she said, "I'm not sure I do."

"Oh, you do so," he said. "I was your best patient ever." She rolled her eyes at that. Just as he went to lift his teacup, his phone rang. "Hey Fallon, what's up?"

"You have a visitor."

He slowly lowered his tea. "Where?"

"Just got on the elevator."

"Recognize him?"

"Yeah. Looks like the good doctor is paying a house call."

She heard the words, even as the shock reverberated in her head.

CHAPTER 16

IS HE SERIOUS? Leia bolted to her feet and stared at the door.

"Get away from the window," Bullard said immediately.

Just as quickly, she pulled him back from the window as well, then turned to look at him. "Where do we go?"

"We don't go anywhere," he said. "The best place for us is right here. Fallon is coming up behind this guy."

"But we're still right here in the line of fire," she said, reaching up a hand to her forehead. By now, the surface of her braid had dried but the activity of the day had wisps flying around her face. She nervously tucked a few of the longer ones behind her ear, as she realized what this would mean. "I'm really not good with confrontation," she said.

"You don't need to be," he said reassuringly.

She stared at him. "Mine is a world of healing," she said, "not death."

"And that's what makes you different from this guy," he said. "He's an asshole, just out for what he can get and for the pleasure he gets from putting other people in pain."

She nodded slowly. "I'd still rather we caught him somewhere else."

He smiled. "But, with us taking out his gunman, Leo pretty well had to do this on his own because you could have passed along information to another detective almost instantly. Leo's got to put a stop to this now."

That all made sense, and she understood, but, jeez, this was not the type of world she wanted to live in. "And how many attacks do you get at home?" she asked him quietly.

"None," he said. "They all know better than that. The only problem is when people start to take over my business."

"Good luck with that," she said, shaking her head.

"It's the same guy involved in all the attacks on me, and I don't know who it is," he said, "but the same person tried to take out my guys too."

"But you don't know who it is, do you?"

"Not yet," he said, "but I'm starting to get an ugly suspicion."

Staring at him, she tilted her head, watching a scary look on his chiseled features; whoever he was thinking of was making him sick to consider. "And why would you all of a sudden have an idea of who it is?"

"It just occurred to me, and it's somebody I haven't seen in a long time. Yet somebody close and has been at the compound many times. We weren't looking in that direction though."

"And now?"

"Now we need to take a look," he said. "If it's true, it will cause me and others a great deal of pain."

"He's a good friend then?"

"No," he said quietly. "It's worse than that."

She stared at him, but a weird sound at the door diverted their attention. She closed her eyes and wrapped her arms around her chest.

He walked over and whispered against her ear, "Go sit down on the floor in the corner beside the couch and don't say a word, no matter what."

She looked up at him, as he leaned over and kissed her hard. She walked back to the corner he was talking about, her heart pounding, and got down, tucked underneath a small table in front. She was basically hidden, so somebody would have to spend precious minutes to actually find her. She never would have thought about being here or choosing this location, but Bullard had it already planned.

He'd assessed the room and realized where the danger was, right from the beginning, and found where the safest place for her was. She had to appreciate a man who looked after his own. That just brought her mind to the stupid asshole at the door, trying to take her life away again. Isn't it bad enough he'd tried three times already?

And, with Bullard standing back, they listened for more sounds at the door. Sure enough, it didn't take long, and there was a *click*, and the door popped open.

How could that be? He must have a master key. She waited and watched carefully, but, from her hidden spot, she couldn't see anything, and all she heard was her unsteady breathing and the slamming of her heart against her chest. She didn't know where Bullard had hidden, but she presumed he was in the open closet behind the door. He was a big man, so it's not like he could just melt into nothing. She waited and heard soft footsteps. As her heart pounded against her chest, she stared around, crunched up as tiny as she could be, and heard the gunman swear.

"Fucking hell, where is she?"

And she closed her eyes, hoping against hope that he wouldn't find her.

"Goddammit. They had to have come back here," he muttered. When he found the connecting door locked, he quickly unlocked it, and it still wouldn't budge, so he slammed his shoulder against it and rushed through. Almost immediately, she heard gunfire and swearing. Her eyes still closed, and her body crunched up as small as she could get, suddenly she heard that condescending voice.

"Well, there you are," he said, with a sneer.

She looked up to see him pointing a handgun at her, with a big long silencer at the end. "What did you do to the other man?" she cried out, slowly rising.

"I didn't do anything," he said. "I was only swearing because I expected to find you in there, but the place was empty. Looks like they deserted you, sweetheart. Men will always desert you because you're nothing. You're absolutely nothing in the world of men or anywhere else."

She stared at him. "Are you really that simple?" she asked him, curiously studying him and wondering what a psych evaluation would reveal for somebody like him.

He glared at her. "You don't know anything about what makes me tick."

"You like to cause chaos and pain. You like to be paid for your work, and you like to do things right under people's noses, so you can be so all-powerful without them knowing."

He looked at her, surprised, and said, "That's not half bad. Maybe you should have gone into psychiatry instead of surgery."

"I am an excellent surgeon," she said.

"Well, I couldn't have some young upstart girl developing new techniques and trying to show me up in my own hospital, could I?"

"I guess not," she said, knowing her phone sat here recording everything. It was on video, something she had started before she'd gone under the table. "So what's the deal? You'll just kill me now?"

"That was my thought, yes," he said. "I highly doubt that your knights in shining armor will be back anytime soon."

"Why is that?"

"Why would they?" he said, sounding surprised. "You're nothing to write home about. Besides, what have you been doing all these years? Look at yourself. You've turned into some sort of peasant girl."

"Living in paradise," she said, with a smile. "It was a hell of a lot better than working in hell with you."

He laughed at that. "And it'll stay that way too. Only this time you'll go to a different little piece of heaven, so to speak."

As he raised the handgun, she straightened and looked directly at him. "I'm not afraid of you."

"I don't care if you're afraid or not." He shrugged. "I just want you gone. You've been a pain in my ass for a long time," he said. "It's too bad you surfaced. We wouldn't have to do this if you hadn't."

He raised the gun, and a shot fired. She stared, shocked as he slowly sagged to the floor. She raced over, but Bullard beat her to it, kicking the gun free. She dropped down to see that it was only a shoulder wound.

"Why did he drop like that? It's just a shoulder wound," she said, noting Leo was silent, mostly in shock for the moment.

"Well, I shot him in the shoulder, but Fallon shot him in the knee." With that, she turned to see that Leo's knee had exploded from whatever Fallon had used as a weapon. She stared at the two bullet wounds. "So he'll live?" But then she answered her own question herself. "Yes, of course he will," she said. "Just for a moment there I wondered."

"No," Bullard said. "You're right to wonder because a guy like this? All he'll do is cause more chaos."

"Well, we have an awful lot about him killing his patients, so, as long as he goes to jail for the rest of his natural life, I guess I'm okay with that too. Hopefully in maximum security—or even solitary confinement sounds great to me." She smiled and said, "Do you want to call the detective?"

"He's already been called," Bullard said, "and he should be coming up the elevator right now."

She looked at Fallon in surprise, then asked Bullard, "What did you do? Go open the door and let Fallon in?"

"Sure did," he said. "I had to leave you alone for the barest of seconds, but I counted on Leo's ego."

"You took a chance," she said, staring down at Leo, who even now moaned on the floor.

He opened his eyes just then and glared at her. "You stupid bitch."

"Yeah, why is that?"

"You should have stayed away," he said. "None of this would have had to happen. Now I'll have to ruin you."

"You think so?" She looked at Bullard and said, "Have you got that recording handy?" He pulled it out and pressed Play, so the doctor heard his own words on the tape recording from five years ago.

Leo's gaze widened. "You fucking bitch," he roared, then groaned with pain. "Where did you get that? It will never be allowed in court!"

"Why not?" she said. "I mean, by the time I put it on the news, I'm pretty sure everybody'll know anyway." He started screaming for real at that point. She walked over to Bullard and said, "Can we go home now?"

"I think that's a great idea," he said. "Are you ready?"

"As ready as I'll ever be," she said, with a smile. "But it's hard to say. You'll have to show me what your world looks like. You saw parts of mine. At least you saw the good parts. This guy, well, he's just part of the old part."

"He's history already," he said. "Don't even worry about him. But I'd love to take you home and show you my world."

"Except for the fact that you just now thought about who it is who may be after you."

At that, Fallon turned and looked at Bullard in surprise. "Do you think you know who it is?"

"I'm afraid so," he said. "I'm hoping I'm wrong, but I'm running out of options." He turned his head and looked at her and then at Fallon. "I have to get home and find out first."

"And what will going home allow you to do?" she asked. "Don't you want to make sure first?"

"Oh, I'll start some investigation right now," he said. "It just occurred to me a few minutes before this guy walked in. I'll get Ice on it."

"You won't let any of us help?" Fallon asked him quietly. "Do you suspect us?"

Bullard looked at him in surprise. "God no," he said. "I know it's none of us. But in a way it's almost closer than that."

Fallon stared at him in confusion. "I don't think there is anything closer than us," he said. "Actually we wondered for the longest time if it was Deedee."

"It wasn't," he said.

"At least she wasn't part of it at the end," Fallon said, "though we don't know if she could have been involved in any way at the beginning or not."

"I would hope not," Bullard said.

"Unfortunately she's already dead, so there's nothing we can do about it anyway," Fallon said.

"I know," Bullard said, "but I'm pretty damn sure that this is somebody who doesn't have anything to do with my business but does have a lot to do with my life, or at least he used to. But I really want to be wrong, so I don't want to accuse him until we know for sure."

"So how will you know for sure?" Leia asked.

"We'll go home," he said. "And, if I'm right, we'll find out almost immediately when we get there."

BULLARD DIDN'T WANT to share his suspicions because it wasn't fair to the person he was thinking of. But there had been just the two of them for so long that it really broke his heart to think it was even possible. But this guy had the training, he had the insight, he had the access to Bullard's compound. And he knew Bullard's men. He knew how to get into the schedule and to do a lot of the IT work because he'd been right there with Bullard for a long time.

And Bullard desperately wanted to be wrong. But, in his heart, he knew he wasn't wrong, and that would be one of the hardest things for him to deal with. But he couldn't know for sure, not yet.

Twenty-four hours later they touched down at the compound. Poor Leia looked more than a little exhausted, after she'd spent hours answering more questions for the detective, while the doctor screamed about how she tried to kill him. But the doctor could scream as much as he wanted; he'd been caught on the hotel cameras with a weapon in his hand, all dressed in black, heading to her hotel room.

And Bullard figured that, once they tracked down the money Leo got from the victims' families, Leo would do everything he could to scream, but nobody would let him wiggle free. And, if that was how it turned out, that's the way it should be. Bullard would just as soon have killed Leo, and maybe they should have, but, if they ever crossed paths again—if this guy ever got free and came after her—Bullard would deep-six Leo in a heartbeat. He needed her to know that she was safe from now on.

As they finally drove into the compound, the front doors opened, and women came flying out. Women and men. Bullard stopped, tears in his eyes, as Izzie and Lindsey both threw themselves into his arms. Both of them bawling. He held them close, knowing that Leia had no clue who these women were. But his family was large and expansive, and his heart was big.

As soon as he could, he stepped back, pulled Leia up close, and introduced her. The other women immediately wrapped their arms around her and sincerely gave her their thanks. Leia was stunned. She looked at him and frowned, clearly puzzled.

"Dave's niece and my niece," he said. Her eyes widened, and she nodded. And just when he thought the world had calmed down a bit, and he felt the emotion of being home choking in the back of his throat, he looked up to see Ice. She walked toward him, with that gorgeous smile that he could never forget. He opened his arms, and she walked into them, and they held each other close. When he opened his arms this time, he turned and wrapped one right around Leia and pulled her up close again.

"Ice, this is Leia."

Ice looked at her and gave her the gentlest of hugs. "You

have my eternal gratitude for saving this man," she said in that beautiful voice of hers.

Leia looked at her closely and then saw something that made her relax. "No," she said, "you saved him for me all these years, and, for that, I am very grateful to you."

Momentarily stunned with surprise, Ice stared and then nodded. "Agreed. Now you have to take care of him. He works way too hard. He won't look after himself, and he cares far too much about everybody else but himself."

As he tried to protest, the two women just smiled in agreement.

Leia said, "Not a problem. I can handle that from here."

Ice nodded and said, "So I hear you're a damn fine surgeon."

"Well, I was."

"You still are," Ice said calmly. "Just wait 'til you see his medical setup."

"And you," Leia asked. "Did you come alone?"

"No," she said, "my better half is here too somewhere."

They all turned, and Bullard saw Levi walking outside, talking with Dave, their voices animated, as they were discussing some kind of new techno system. Bullard took one look at Levi and reached out, and the two men hugged.

"Damn it, Bullard, if you ever pull some kind of a shit-storm like that again, I—"

Bullard burst out laughing, his world so damn complete, he thought he had died and gone to heaven. "Man, I didn't know if I would ever get back here again," he said.

Dave turned and said, "Your brother, he's here too. It was a hell of a trip, but he refused to stay away."

At that, something inside Bullard stilled, and he nodded slowly. "Where is he?"

"Inside, playing with the electronics," Dave said. "He

just got here though. We'll all need some coffee and a chance to catch up."

"Indeed," Bullard said. As they walked inside, he held Leia close, and Ice looked on with a big smile. He knew that she was happy for him, and honestly he could now put that all to rest. Leia was both as different yet as similar as he could possibly have found. And, damn, he had chosen well. He looked down at Leia and kissed her gently on the cheek. "Welcome home."

She rolled her eyes at him. "It's not a Pacific island."

He walked her through the massive stone building out to the big pool and the surrounding areas and said, "It's not a Pacific island," he said, "but anything you want to change to make you feel more at home," he said, "I'm all for it."

She stared at the big pool and the huge expansive gardens. "This is beautiful," she said. "Who did this?"

"I designed it, and Dave looks after it," he said. "It's actually been the balm for our broken hearts for a long time," he said, with a laugh.

"It's stunning," she murmured, as she walked closer and looked like she couldn't believe it. She turned and said, "You are a lucky man."

"I am," he said, beaming, as he pulled her back into his arms and kissed her gently. "Not the least of which is that you found me and brought me back to health," he said.

She shook her head. "You'll have to get over that soon," she said. "I won't let you keep touting all that gratitude stuff."

"Okay," he said. "I'll deal with that but just not at the moment." He turned and led her to the big command center area.

She stood and whistled. "Wow," she said, "this is incredible."

CHAPTER 17

L EIA COULDN'T BELIEVE it; this place was beyond gorgeous. To think that Bullard had created this for himself was just hard to believe. He was clearly a man of great artistic talents. She knew she'd be quite happy here, particularly if she didn't have to travel very much. It wasn't to her liking, as her stomach was still a little on the unsettled side. She walked around the massive room to find another man, looking similar to Bullard, with a big smile on his face. She held out her hand and said, "Hi, I'm Leia."

"Of course," he said, "my brother gets shot out of the air and lands on a deserted island, only to be rescued by a beautiful woman." He shook his head. "Damn," he said, "a pretty nice way to go."

Bullard appeared almost immediately, his smile broad, though his gaze was watchful.

"I'm Blachard."

"Shot out of the air? Is that what happened?" Bullard asked Blachard.

His brother looked at him in surprise. "I thought that's what you guys said happened."

Fallon and Ryland immediately stepped up.

"Well, we didn't say that," Ryland said, then looked at Dave.

"I certainly didn't say that," Dave said, slowly shaking

his head. "I haven't said anything like that at all."

"My bad," Blachard said bashfully. "I assumed that's how they got you."

"And here we thought it was a bomb on the plane," Bullard said.

"Well, the small jet didn't have the ability to track things like rockets," Ryland said. "But shot out of the air would explain the sudden explosion, wouldn't it?" He moved ever-so-slightly closer, as Blachard stepped back.

"Hey, hey, hey. It was just a simple mistake," he said. "I didn't mean anything by it."

"No, of course not," Leia said calmly, as she studied him for a long moment. "You know," she said. "When I was out looking around and fishing, I found him," she said. "I didn't even think he was alive. So, whoever did this to him really didn't want to see him live."

"Hey, don't look at me," Blachard said. "I just can't believe he survived. We owe you our greatest thanks."

"Sure," she said noncommittally, but, as she studied one brother, then the other, she realized that Bullard wasn't comfortable at all. She followed that train of thought but wasn't sure how she could trick the man into saying more. And then she thought back.

"You know what? A ship was out in the ocean at the time," she said, "and there was talk about something in the water. I can't even remember what it was." She frowned, thinking about it. "I remember. It was almost like an asteroid or something. It didn't even occur to me that it was a rocket."

"You saw it?" Bullard asked, staring at her.

"I'm not sure," she said. "It wasn't that day. It was like the previous night—or maybe the previous day. I don't know," she said. "You know what it's like on island time. I remember seeing something shoot through the sky and then an explosion. Maybe that's why I went fishing that day. I did see a lot of parts and pieces, but it was far away. I just kept going. I want to think that, deep inside, I knew, but there is no way to know for sure."

"It's okay," Bullard said.

"But then I found you, and I never really thought about it again."

"I don't know anybody who would have had access to rockets," Bullard said. "I mean, obviously I do, and we have contacts who certainly would have access." And then he slowly looked at his brother. "Bro, that's something you would have known too."

"Hey, I had nothing to do with it," he said, his hands up. "This is starting to sound like an inquest, but I'm just here to catch up on the reunion. I haven't been here in forever, and Ice has been keeping me up to date with the news and all."

"But you were here a little bit ago," Izzie said.

He looked at her in surprise. "No, I wasn't," he said.

"Yes. Yes, you were," she said. "I remember seeing you outside the gate."

"When?" he asked, but there was an edginess to his voice.

Fallon stepped up behind him.

"Whoa, whoa, whoa," Blachard said. "What the hell is this?"

"What this is," Leia said quietly, "looks like betrayal, some of the worst betrayal ever."

"What do you know about it?" he said, with a sneer.

"I know all about betrayal," she said. "But I don't necessarily understand what your role is in all this."

"Nothing," he said. "I didn't have a role in this at all."

But Bullard said, "You knew Deedee. You actually had an affair with her," he said. "You knew the guys who worked for her, and she had access to a whole number of assassins all down the line."

"So do many others," Blachard said, his voice hard and his hands on his hips. Yet he had that look of a cornered rat.

Leia stared at him in shock. "You did it," she said. "You actually did it. You shot down their plane and set all this in motion. You are responsible for all these men who had been injured or nearly died. How could you do that?"

He stared at her, his jaw working, as he figured out what to say.

When Bullard stepped forward, he asked, "Why? Why are you doing this? I see the hate in your actions, and yet I don't know what I did to deserve it."

His brother turned, his face twisting into a vile expression of evil, as he sneered at them. "Five years. *Five long hellish years* while you got to live a life as a free man, while you supposedly were looking for me. Like hell. You took your sweet time with that, didn't you?"

Bullard's face twisted in shock.

"If it had been any of your team, you'd have found them in no time. No, me, your half brother, you were content to let me rot in a cell. I thought of nothing else all those long cold months in solitary. I knew you would tell everyone you were looking but would make me suffer. Well, I planned to make you suffer as soon as I could. It took a while to set up, but, once I did, I realized I could have it all at the same time. Your company *and* Kingdom Securities. Hell, Ice is a great friend. I could take out Levi and have her too."

Bullard struggled to see through the rage in his heart and his mind as he studied his broken brother. The years as a prisoner had done more damage than he had suspected. But no one would have guessed this. ... Who could?

Izzie stepped forward. "Dad?"

His face worked, as he stared at his daughter. "And you," he sneered. "You always preferred him to me."

Her jaw dropped. "He looked after me when you disappeared. You were gone for five years, then suddenly showed up, a changed man," she said. "You've barely spoken to me in years!"

"I was putting things in motion," he said. "Your uncle here would say that I had gone away to lick my wounds," he said, "but what I was doing was making plans."

"What plans?" she asked. "To get back at him? Please don't tell me that's what you were doing."

He glared at her. "What do you care? You'll just hook up with one of his team members anyway. You'll never be number one."

"I don't need to be number one. I just want to be a good person and to live a decent life," she said. "But look at you. All you've done is hurt people."

He sneered at her. "And again, you don't understand. You're just like your mother."

She stiffened at that. "I'll take that as a compliment, thank you."

He laughed. "Take it however you want, all of you. Because it really doesn't make any difference anymore." And, with that, he pulled out a hand grenade, snapping the top off in front of them. Everybody's gaze was locked on to that grenade. If he dropped it, they would all go up.

Bullard looked at him and said, "Seriously? You're willing to take what fifteen, twenty people to their deaths, including yourself and your own daughter?"

"If you let me go," he said, "I'll disappear again."

"What? So you can run away and hide, making plans to come back and try to kill all my men and shoot my plane out of the air ... again?"

"It cost me a lot of money to set that up," he said. "How typical that you survived. You're one of those goddamn golden boys who never ever fails, no matter what it is."

"Oh, I failed a lot," he said quietly. "But not at this. I've dedicated my life to this work," he said. "But I can't fathom spending one ounce of energy to get back at somebody I cared about."

"I haven't cared about you since we were little," he said, "since it became obvious to all that you were bigger and better, like a bright shiny penny for everyone around." He said it with so much bitterness that everybody just stared at him.

Ice stepped forward and said, "Blachard, is that really how you want to play this out right now?"

"Why not?" he said. "He even comes back from the dead with a gorgeous woman in love with him. Who else does that?" he said, shaking his head. "If I drop this right now, it's all over for everyone. And I, for one, am totally okay with that."

"Well, I don't think anybody else is," Bullard said.

Leia took a quick look around, and she saw the men assessing options, but it was all about that grenade. She didn't know very much, but she knew that one of the men in the back of Bullard had a metal box with a lid on it. She looked at the grenade, looked at the box, and reached out a hand behind Bullard's back. The metal box quickly made its way up to the front. Once she had it in her hand, she looked down at it. "I presume a grenade like that should go into a box like this, huh?"

Blachard looked at it and laughed. "But it'll never happen," he said. "I'll drop it instead, and it'll go off, like crazy."

"Maybe," she said, "or maybe you just want to put it in here." She took two steps forward, holding out the box.

"And why would I want to do that?" he asked, staring at her like she was a snake.

"Because the one thing that you really don't want to do is die yourself."

"I'll die anyway. The minute they get a chance, every one of the men in this room will try to kill me."

"You're right," she said.

And he pulled out something from the back of his pocket. It was small, metal.

And she recognized it. "A scalpel," she said. "Are you a surgeon too?"

"Of course not," he said, "but it's sharp, and it makes a hell of a weapon."

"It does"—she smiled—"but it won't be a weapon you can use if you don't put that grenade in here."

"I don't give a shit," he said, and then he grabbed her and held the scalpel against her neck.

She sighed. "You know that's really not an answer either." She held out the box, even as he pressed his scalpel against her neck, and she felt the pinch. "Put the grenade in here."

He thought about it and then said, "Hell no. I've got both. I'll get out of here with you, and I'll find another way to leave the country."

"You're not going anywhere." She held the box underneath the grenade, not worried about the scalpel at her neck. She was more worried about ensuring that, when the guys took their shot, the grenade would fall into the open metal case. She looked up at Bullard and said, "I think it's a really good time to count."

An inaudible hum rose as everyone silently counted down together.

Three ...

Two ...

And it was so silent, but she heard it in her head. As soon as they got to one, she slammed the box up to the grenade, as the bullets were fired.

Blachard's head took the bulk of the hits, and he immediately released the grenade, which dropped into the box. She stepped around the scalpel still in his hand, as he fell to the floor. But she held the grenade in the box in her hand. She handed it to Fallon. "I hope you can dispose of that."

He took it from her and, with a voice filled with respect, said, "Yes, ma'am, I sure can," and quickly he disappeared. She turned to look down at Blachard and said, "No surgery needed here." Damn glad to have all this over, she knew recovery wouldn't be as easy or as fast for Bullard this time, but she could help there too. Bending down, she pulled the scalpel from his hand, looked at it, and said, "Wow, this is one of the better ones. Did he steal it from your surgery center?"

Bullard nodded, as he snatched her up into his arms, where she cuddled in close.

"I think I'd like to see that surgery suite now," she said, "because this is one of the best brands, and I'm all about good equipment."

He shook his head, chuckling. "You know I'm totally

okay too," he said in relief. "Let me see to Izzie, and then we'll get the hell out of here, so the guys can take care of this."

"Revenge, greed, money, and jealousy," she said. "That's all it ever is."

After seeing that Quinn had Izzie well in hand, Bullard led Leia into the surgery suite.

She stopped and stared, as Bullard pointed out all the equipment she could have at her fingertips, if she wanted to. "But this is better than in any of the hospitals I've ever seen." Her heart swelled in joy at the gleaming equipment.

"Remember that thing about money?" he said, with a lopsided grin.

She smiled and said, "Now this could be a pleasure."

"It will be a pleasure," he said; then he walked closer and snatched her into his arms again, as if he were afraid that she would somehow disappear. "Don't you ever pull a stunt like that again. You scared me half to death."

"I won't have to," she said, "if you will stop creating so many enemies. Remember? The most dangerous enemies are nearly always from within."

He held her close. "I know," he whispered, "but no longer."

CHAPTER 18

LATER THAT NIGHT, after several glasses of wine and a solid meal that Dave had produced almost magically from the massive kitchen, Bullard led her upstairs to his bedroom.

"What? I don't get my own bedroom?" she said in a teasing voice.

"You can have anything you want," he said, "as long as you stay with me." There was such a note of vulnerability in his voice that she turned and kissed him gently and said, "I have no intention of going anywhere else. But I will insist on dragging you back to the islands every once in a while."

"And I promise we'll go," he said. "I really do think we should buy up a bunch of land and keep it for a retreat for all of us."

"That would be lovely," she said, throwing her arms around him and giving him a big kiss. "As long as we're together, I'll be fine."

He dropped his gaze, then held her close and kissed her gently.

She shook her head. "Oh no, you don't, no need to be so gentle," she said. "I've waited far too long for this." She kissed him back, passion rippling through her body and curling her toes, pressing her body as tightly against him as she could.

He was already there, holding her against him, his body already at attention, as he wrapped his arms around her, picked her up, and carried her to his massive bed. When he laid her down on the bed, he whispered to her, "You know something? I can almost see why my brother was so upset, and how bringing you home was like the final straw."

"I don't give a shit about your brother," she said, bouncing off the bed to quickly shed the little bit of clothing she had on, then stood before him in her honey-kissed skin from the island.

He just stared, shook his head, and said, "I'm one damn lucky man."

"You're one very overdressed man," she said and quickly put her hands on his belt buckle to help him out of his jeans.

He laughed and stripped down almost as fast as she had. He wrapped her in his arms, and, laying her on the bed again, he whispered, "Mine?"

She nodded. "All yours." Then she wrapped her arms around his neck and whispered, "Mine?"

He nodded. "Yours forever."

It certainly didn't take very long for the tears to come to her eyes, and she realized just how much this man meant to her. But he wouldn't have any of it. With the passion still rising between them, he cuddled and caressed and kissed until she was mindless with joy, her heart overwhelmed with love, and her body just waiting for possession.

"Hurry," she said, "I can't wait another minute."

He said, "No way, I want to make it last."

"We could make it last," she said, "later, much later."

He chuckled and settled himself between her thighs, and, when she looked up, he laced his fingers in hers, raised her arms over her head, and slowly entered her. She twisted and moaned underneath him. "Dear God," she said, "it's been so long."

"Good," he said, with a note of satisfaction. "I can't even remember anybody else but you," he said.

"And that's the way it should be," she whispered, and finally he was seated right to the hilt. *Home.* And that's what she felt like, that she had come home.

She whispered, as she pulled him closer, "It feels like a homecoming right now." Then he started to move, and she realized that, although everything had been perfect, it would get so much better. By the time he finally tossed them over the edge, she was screaming, mindless with joy, her body trembling beneath him. When he rolled over to the side and pulled her up close against him, she was trembling every-where.

"Are you okay?" he asked tenderly.

"I'm fine," she answered, when she could. "I'm so damn fine."

"You don't look like it," he said bluntly. "I'm scared I've hurt you."

She tilted her head back to look up at him, even as her shakes calmed down. "When you haven't done something like this before, and you're overwhelmed with passion and emotion and love," she said, "this is what happens."

"Just so long as you're okay." Then rolling over, he pulled her close and whispered, "And anytime you want to return to your island, just say the word."

"And you'll drop everything and make it happen?" she asked, a twinkle in her eye.

"I promise."

"And you promise that you'll come with me, every time?"

"That's a deal," he said and pulled her close.

She smiled, tucked in closer, and said, "Actually the island would be a great place for a wedding."

He nodded, looked down at her, and said, "Or we can do it here."

"We could," she said. "I'll have to think about it."

"You do that," he said, "and, yes, if need be, the wedding can be at the island."

She chuckled and said, "We'll talk about it tomorrow." Then snuggling in, she closed her eyes and slept.

Her heart, mind, and soul, for once, were at total peace beside her gentle warrior.

EPILOGUE

I T WOULDN'T BE the easiest thing to get everybody to the
island, but everybody wanted to attend, so that's how the
plans were laid out now. Even Levi and Ice were coming,
toddler in tow, and so was all of Bullard's crew, with all their
women too. It had been Leia's decision to return here and to
say goodbye to the island temporarily, but also to say hello to
her new life. She had friends on the island, she hadn't had a
chance to say goodbye to, and new friends she wanted to
introduce to such a lovely place. So the entire entourage
would be here eventually.

In the back of Bullard's mind, he couldn't help but
think that somebody there had betrayed her. Somebody had
told the outside world that they were there on the island, so
it still may not be quite the place that she expected it to be.
So Bullard still had to find that snitch. But he was willing to
go along with Leia's plans for her island wedding. They
would be here for two weeks, with his team coming and
going in the meantime. At least that's what it looked like at
the moment.

At that thought, Fallon walked over to the pool to join
Bullard, and so did Ryland and Kano.

"So it's your special day," Fallon said.

Bullard nodded. "Well, next week is, yes. Why?" He
looked at them, and the three men looked at each other and

shrugged. "Come on. Spit it out," Bullard said.

"Well," Ryland said, "we were actually wondering if you might enjoy a bigger wedding than you had initially planned."

Bullard frowned.

"Or if you needed it for just yourselves?"

"What are you talking about?" Bullard asked.

"We all have some shy lady friends, being a little too slow about getting up to the altar," Kano said. "Lots and lots of promises about forever, but we wondered about putting them on the spot and having one big joint wedding ceremony."

Bullard grinned, then chuckled, then laughed uproariously. "I'm okay with multiple weddings," he said. "I'm just not sure about putting your ladyloves on the spot."

"I think that," Fallon said, "once we present the idea of an island wedding, we might get more than we bargained for. At least I'm hoping so."

Bullard looked at him and said, "Are you actually expecting to get your lady friend up to the altar with you? You too?" he asked, looking at Ryland and at Kano. All three men nodded. "Well, let's just do a wedding for everyone then," Bullard said.

"I overheard the women say something about it should be your day," Kano noted.

"I don't care about that, but maybe it should be Leia's day," Bullard said, with a frown. "I suppose you want this to be a secret?" The guys nodded. "So how about our wedding happens solo, and you guys stay afterward to have your big mass weddings right afterward—or even the next day?"

"As long as you're open to it, we may discuss it among ourselves," Ryland said. "The minister will be there for more than a day anyway."

"True."

They all thought about it for a long moment.

"Change of subject," Kano said. "Did anybody consider the fact that somebody from the island must have leaked or even sold information to the outside world?"

Bullard nodded. "I am worried about that," he said. "I don't think it'll be a big deal, but we may have to stop some gossip and the media."

"And that's likely a leak from the island too, right?"

"Yes, I would think so," he said. "I don't want anything to ruin her wedding."

"Right. So we'll have to look into that," the men said. Looking at each other, Ryland said, "Damn. It still sounds like a fun holiday though."

"And one we all need," Fallon said, with that confident certainty in his tone. "Now that you're settled, Bullard, I'd love to see Dave find somebody."

"I would too," Bullard said. "He's been alone for a long time."

"Well, we'll see. Everybody's been very lucky so far," Fallon said. At that, the men were willing to leave it.

As Bullard walked away, he thought about having all the weddings on the island and realized it could be a hell of a nice thing for everyone. Then he thought about Dave and the caterer who he had used to see off and on. Bullard was pretty damn sure that Dave was a big fan of the caterer still, but the two of them had been slow to pull things together— most likely Dave being the stumbling block. Maybe this could be something that would push them closer. As Bullard walked into the compound's kitchen, Dave was there with a long list.

"Everybody'll be on the island," Dave said. "We'll have to haul in a fair bit of groceries."

"What about your caterer?"

"Yep, she'll go," Dave said, "with a lot of food that she can finish on board the boat and bring over, in case there are no cooking facilities."

"There aren't any cooking facilities," Bullard said cheerfully. "Yet people manage to cook and eat just fine."

Dave rolled his eyes. "You never make it easy, do you?"

"Leia wants it simple."

"Yeah, Katie said something about that, and she's talked to Leia a couple times."

"Yeah, so how are things with you and Katie?"

Dave looked up, a flush high on his cheeks. "We've worked together fine over the years," he said, "and she knows the area well, which is a blessing."

"So you are in touch with her often?"

"Haven't been for a while, but she heard you were missing and called me," he said, nodding. "It's been nice to have somebody to talk to through the last few months of chaos."

"Right," Bullard said. "Well, let's see how this next step of our life goes."

"First, we have to get you married," Dave said, with a laugh.

"About that, there's a chance," he said, "that some of the men might try to get married too. Maybe even as a surprise to all the women."

Dave stared at him. "Jesus," he said, "that would be a hell of a thing to pull off."

"It would," Bullard said, with a smile. "And would it be possible to pull it off without having all our lives in danger?"

At that, Dave frowned, shook his head, and said, "You

know something? I'd like to say yes, but I think it's a no."

Bullard nodded. "I'm afraid you're right," he said. "I know that this is what Leia really wants, and that's what we'll do, but I feel very much like something else is going on here. Something that goes back to the island."

"Then let's go back and deal with it," Dave said. "With all of us there, it's a whole different story than just the two of you."

"Got it," Bullard said. "So let's make it happen."

"Make what happen exactly?" Dave asked, frowning.

Bullard grinned, and, with his arms spread wide, he said, "All of it! The wedding for us, a wedding for everyone else, and making sure we stop whoever it is who betrayed Leia on the island before."

"Right," Dave said. "You're asking for a lot."

"Nope," Bullard replied. "I'm asking for the moon. Not a problem. We've done that before, so let's do it again."

This concludes Book 8 of Bullard's Battle: Bullard's Beauty.

Read about Bullard's Best: Bullard's Battle, Book 9

Bullard's Best: Bullard's Battle (Book #9)

Welcome to a new stand-alone but interconnected series from Dale Mayer. This is Bullard's story—and that of his team's. All raw, rough, incredibly capable men who have one goal: to find out who was behind the attack on their leader, before the attacker, or attackers, return to finish the job.

Stay tuned for more nonstop action as the men narrow down their suspects … and find a way to let love back into their own empty lives.

After finding the killer who'd tried to take out the entire team, and now with Bullard safe, the crew heads back to the island where he recovered. Leia wants to get married there, so Dave has gone ahead with Katie, Bullard's caterer, to set things up.

Dave has a new lease on life, now that Bullard is safely back home, and fixes his sights on an old friend he's always kept slightly distant. Katie has been in Dave's orbit for a long time; she's not sure what's changed in their relationship, but something certainly has, and she couldn't be happier.

Except for one loose thread from that same island. After all, someone let the outside world know Bullard was alive. Someone they had yet to find. So a week in paradise might start with some time in hell first.

Find Book 9 here!

To find out more visit Dale Mayer's website.

smarturl.it/DMSBest

Damon's Deal: Terkel's Team (Book #1)

Welcome to a brand-new series from *USA Today* best-selling author Dale Mayer, where dark-ops SEALs have special senses and skills, needed to solve intrigue, betrayal, and … murder. A series with all the elements you've come to love, plus so much more, … including psychics!

ICE POURED HERSELF a coffee and sat down at the compound's massive dining room table with the others. When her phone rang, she smiled at the number displayed. "Hey, Terk. How're you doing?" She put the call on Speakerphone.

"I'm okay," Terkel said, his voice distracted and tight.

"Terk?" Merk called from across the table. He got up and walked closer and sat across from Levi. "You don't sound too good, brother. What's up?"

"I'm fine," Terk said. "Or I will be. Right now, things are blown to shit."

"As in literally?" Merk asked.

"The entire group," Terk said, "they're all gone. I had a

solid team of eight, and they're all gone."

"Dead?"

Several others stood to join them, gathered around Ice's phone. Levi stepped forward, his hand on Ice's shoulder. "Terk? Are they all dead?"

"No." Terk took a deep breath. "I'm not making sense. I'm sorry."

"Take it easy," Ice said, her voice calm and reassuring. "What do you mean, *they're all gone?*"

"All their abilities are gone," he said. "Something's happened to them. Somebody has deliberately removed whatever super senses they could utilize—or what we have been utilizing for the last ten years for the government." His tone was bitter. "When the US gov recently closed us down, they promised that our black ops department would never rise again, but I didn't expect them to attack us personally."

"What are you talking about?" Merk said in alarm, standing up now to stare at Ice's phone. "Are you in danger?"

"Maybe? I don't know," Terk said. "I need to find out exactly what the hell's going on."

"What can we do to help?" Ice asked.

Terk gave a broken laugh. "That's not why I'm calling. Well, it is, but it isn't."

Ice looked at Merk, who frowned, as he shook his head. Ice knew he and the others had heard Terk's stressed out tone and the completely confusing bits and pieces coming from his mouth. Ice said, "Terk, you're not making sense again. Take a breath and explain. Please. You're scaring me."

Terk took a long slow deep breath. "Tell Stone to open the gate," he said. "She's out there."

"Who's out there?" Levi asked, hopped up, looked outside, and shrugged.

"She's coming up the road now. You have to let her in."

"Who? Why?"

"*Because*," he said, "she's also harnessed with C-4."

"Jesus," Levi said, bolting to display the camera feeds to the big screen in the room. "Is it live?"

"It is, and she's been sent to you."

"Well, that's an interesting move," Ice said, her voice sharp, activating her comm to connect to Stone in the control room. "Who's after us?"

"I think it's rebels within the Iranian government. But it could be our own government. I don't know anymore," Terk snapped. "I also don't know how they got her so close to you. Or how they pinned your connection to me," he said. "I've been very careful."

"We can look after ourselves," Ice said immediately. "But who is this woman to you?"

"She's pregnant," he said, "so that adds to the intensity here."

"Understood. So who is the father? Is he connected somehow?"

There was silence on the other end.

Merk said, "Terk, talk to us."

"She's carrying my baby," Terk replied, his voice heavy.

Merk, his expression grim, looked at Ice, her face mirroring his shock. He asked, "How do you know her, Terk?"

"Brother, you don't understand," Terk said. "I've never met this woman before in my life." And, with that, the phone went dead.

Find Book 1 here!

To find out more visit Dale Mayer's website.

smarturl.it/DMSTTDamon

Author's Note

Thank you for reading Bullard's Beauty: Bullard's Battle, Book 8! If you enjoyed the book, please take a moment and leave a short review.

Dear reader,

I love to hear from readers, and you can contact me at my website: www.dalemayer.com or at my Facebook author page. To be informed of new releases and special offers, sign up for my newsletter or follow me on BookBub. And if you are interested in joining Dale Mayer's Reader Group, here is the Facebook sign up page.
https://smarturl.it/DaleMayerFBGroup

Cheers,
Dale Mayer

Get THREE Free Books Now!

Have you met the SEALS of Honor?

SEALs of Honor Books 1, 2, and 3. Follow the stories of brave, badass warriors who serve their country with honor and love their women to the limits of life and death.

Read Mason, Hawk, and Dane right now for FREE.

Go here and tell me where to send them!
http://smarturl.it/EthanBofB

About the Author

Dale Mayer is a *USA Today* best-selling author, best known for her SEALs military romances, her Psychic Visions series, and her Lovely Lethal Garden cozy series. Her contemporary romances are raw and full of passion and emotion (Broken But … Mending series). Her thrillers will keep you guessing (By Death series), and her romantic comedies will keep you giggling (*It's a Dog's Life*, a stand-alone novella; and the Broken Protocols series, starring Charming Marvin, the cat).

Dale honors the stories that come to her—and some of them are crazy and break all the rules and cross multiple genres!

To go with her fiction, she also writes nonfiction in many different fields, with books available on résumé writing, companion gardening, and the US mortgage system. She has recently published her Career Essentials series. All her books are available in print and ebook format.

Connect with Dale Mayer Online

Dale's Website – www.dalemayer.com
Twitter – @DaleMayer
Facebook – facebook.com/DaleMayer.author
BookBub – bookbub.com/authors/dale-mayer

Also by Dale Mayer

Published Adult Books:

Bullard's Battle
Ryland's Reach, Book 1

Cain's Cross, Book 2

Eton's Escape, Book 3

Garret's Gambit, Book 4

Kano's Keep, Book 5

Fallon's Flaw, Book 6

Quinn's Quest, Book 7

Bullard's Beauty, Book 8

Bullard's Best, Book 9

Terkel's Team
Damon's Deal, Book 1

Kate Morgan
Simon Says... Hide, Book 1

Hathaway House
Aaron, Book 1

Brock, Book 2

Cole, Book 3

Denton, Book 4

The K9 Files

Psychic Vision Series

Tuesday's Child

Hide 'n Go Seek

Maddy's Floor

Garden of Sorrow

Knock Knock...

Rare Find

Eyes to the Soul

Now You See Her

Shattered

Into the Abyss

Seeds of Malice

Eye of the Falcon

Itsy-Bitsy Spider

Unmasked

Deep Beneath

From the Ashes

Stroke of Death

Ice Maiden

Snap, Crackle...

What If...

Psychic Visions Books 1–3

Psychic Visions Books 4–6

Psychic Visions Books 7–9

By Death Series

Touched by Death

Haunted by Death

Chilled by Death

By Death Books 1–3

Broken Protocols – Romantic Comedy Series
Cat's Meow

Cat's Pajamas

Cat's Cradle

Cat's Claus

Broken Protocols 1-4

Broken and... Mending
Skin

Scars

Scales (of Justice)

Broken but... Mending 1-3

Glory
Genesis

Tori

Celeste

Glory Trilogy

Biker Blues
Morgan: Biker Blues, Volume 1

Cash: Biker Blues, Volume 2

SEALs of Honor
Mason: SEALs of Honor, Book 1

Hawk: SEALs of Honor, Book 2

Dane: SEALs of Honor, Book 3

Swede: SEALs of Honor, Book 4

Heroes for Hire

Heroes for Hire, Books 1–3
Heroes for Hire, Books 4–6
Heroes for Hire, Books 7–9
Heroes for Hire, Books 10–12
Heroes for Hire, Books 13–15

SEALs of Steel

Badger: SEALs of Steel, Book 1
Erick: SEALs of Steel, Book 2
Cade: SEALs of Steel, Book 3
Talon: SEALs of Steel, Book 4
Laszlo: SEALs of Steel, Book 5
Geir: SEALs of Steel, Book 6
Jager: SEALs of Steel, Book 7
The Final Reveal: SEALs of Steel, Book 8
SEALs of Steel, Books 1–4
SEALs of Steel, Books 5–8
SEALs of Steel, Books 1–8

The Mavericks

Kerrick, Book 1
Griffin, Book 2
Jax, Book 3
Beau, Book 4
Asher, Book 5
Ryker, Book 6
Miles, Book 7
Nico, Book 8
Keane, Book 9

Lennox, Book 10

Gavin, Book 11

Shane, Book 12

Diesel, Book 13

Jerricho, Book 14

Killian, Book 15

The Mavericks, Books 1–2

The Mavericks, Books 3–4

The Mavericks, Books 5–6

The Mavericks, Books 7–8

The Mavericks, Books 9–10

The Mavericks, Books 11–12

Collections

Dare to Be You…

Dare to Love…

Dare to be Strong…

RomanceX3

Standalone Novellas

It's a Dog's Life

Riana's Revenge

Second Chances

Published Young Adult Books:

Family Blood Ties Series

Vampire in Denial

Vampire in Distress

Vampire in Design

Vampire in Deceit

Vampire in Defiance

Vampire in Conflict

Vampire in Chaos

Vampire in Crisis

Vampire in Control

Vampire in Charge

Family Blood Ties Set 1–3

Family Blood Ties Set 1–5

Family Blood Ties Set 4–6

Family Blood Ties Set 7–9

Sian's Solution, A Family Blood Ties Series Prequel
Novelette

Design series

Dangerous Designs

Deadly Designs

Darkest Designs

Design Series Trilogy

Standalone

In Cassie's Corner

Gem Stone (a Gemma Stone Mystery)

Time Thieves

Published Non-Fiction Books:

Career Essentials

Career Essentials: The Résumé

Career Essentials: The Cover Letter

Career Essentials: The Interview

Career Essentials: 3 in 1

Made in United States
Orlando, FL
04 June 2022

18467136R10141